"We can't do this, Julie."

Hurt suffused her and she pulled away, straightening her clothes. "Why? Because you still blame me? Because I was too rough on your brother?"

Brody pulled her back to him, his eyes smokier than she'd ever seen them. Hunger and need flared in his expression, his breathing as ragged as her own.

"No," he said between clenched teeth. "I meant, we can't do it now." His gaze dropped to her breasts, and her body tingled.

"But we will make love," he said. "I will have you again, because I've never stopped wanting you."

Julie's heart stuttered, a myriad of emotions flooding her throat so she couldn't speak.

"Now, go to bed before I change my mind and take you right here in the hall, and we both know that's not a good idea."

RITA HERRON

ULTIMATE COWBOY

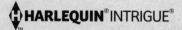

To my fabulous editor Allison for 50 plus books!

Recycling programs for this product may not exist in your area.

ISBN-13: 978-0-373-74722-1

ULTIMATE COWBOY

Copyright © 2013 by Rita B. Herron

HARLEQUIN®

Printed in U.S.A.

™ www.Harlequin.com

ABOUT THE AUTHOR

Award-winning author Rita Herron wrote her first book when she was twelve, but didn't think real people grew up to be writers. Now she writes so she doesn't have to get a *real* job. A former kindergarten teacher and workshop leader, she traded storytelling to kids for writing romance, and now she writes romantic comedies and romantic suspense. She lives in Georgia with her own romance hero and three kids. She loves to hear from readers, so please write her at P.O. Box 921225, Norcross, GA 30092-1225, or visit her website, www.ritaherron.com.

Books by Rita Herron

HARLEQUIN INTRIGUE

CAST OF CHARACTERS

Brody Bloodworth—He has never stopped looking for his little brother, Will, who disappeared seven years ago, but now Special Agent Julie Whitehead, his former girlfriend and lover, has found him. Will Brody get his brother back and have a second chance with Julie?

Special Agent Julie Whitehead—She blamed herself for Will's disappearance and made it her mission to find him and bring him back to Brody. But she can't take a chance on losing her heart to the rugged cowboy again.

Will Bloodworth—He was kidnapped when he was seven years old. Who took him and where has he been all this time?

Kyle Wyle—He gets caught for robbing a convenience store and refuses to talk about his past. Is he really Will?

Tray Goodner—Kyle's accomplice; is Tray his real name?

Alan Mitland—This ex-military man lost his baby while he was deployed. Did he take Will to make up for the son he lost?

Cox Fuller—His wife ran off with his son and left him while he was in the army. Did he abduct Will to replace his son?

Barry Moody—He's suffering from PTSD and is running a meth lab. Could he be the kidnapper who stole Will and nine other boys?

Jeremy Wyle—Is Kyle's brother helping lure other victims to the man they call Father?

Father—He believes he's starting his own army and turning the boys he kidnaps into soldiers. What is his name?

Chapter One

"This special news report just in—an amber alert has been issued for six-year-old Hank Forte. Hank was last seen at the county fair in Amarillo."

Brody Bloodworth's heart clenched as a photo of the boy appeared on screen. The little boy had blond hair, was wearing a black T-shirt, jeans and cowboy boots. He could be one of the kids on the BBL, the Bucking Bronc Lodge he had started for needy children.

But he reminded him more of his own little brother, Will, and launched him back seven years ago to the day Will had gone missing.

Not from a county fair but from the rodeo where *he* was supposed to be watching him.

Self-loathing and guilt suffused him, once again robbing his lungs of air. He understood what the family of that little boy was going through now. The panic. The fear.

The guilt.

If only they'd kept a better eye on him. If only they hadn't turned their head for a minute.

What was happening to him? Had he just wandered off? Would they find him hiding out or playing somewhere at the fair? Maybe he had fallen asleep in a stall housing one of the animals...

Or had someone taken him? Maybe a desperate woman who'd lost a child and was out of her mind? A child predator who'd do God knows what?

A killer?

The reporter turned the microphone to Hank's parents, a couple who were huddled together, teary-eyed and frightened. A second later, they began to plead for their son's return, and the mother broke down into sobs.

Brody hit the remote, silencing the heart-wrenching scene, but it played over and over in his head. But it wasn't the Forte family's cries he heard; it was his own family's.

His father who'd blamed him from the get-go.

Because it was his fault.

He glanced through the window at the sprawling acres and acres of land he'd bought, to the horse stables and pens and the boys that he'd taken in. All kids who had troubles, boys who needed homes and love and guidance.

But no matter how much he did for them, it wouldn't make up for losing his little brother.

The clock in the hall struck 6:00 p.m., and he stood, pulled on his duster jacket and headed outside. One of his best men, Mason Blackpaw, and his fiancée, Cara Winchester, were getting married on the ranch in a few minutes. He'd promised he'd be there, and he was happy for his friend, but weddings always made him uncomfortable.

And he'd attended a hell of a lot of them lately. In fact, all of his original investors had tied the knot. First Johnny Long, then Brandon Woodstock, Carter Flagstone, then Miles McGregor, and now Mason.

Yanking at his tie to loosen the choking knot, he glanced at the field to the right where Mason had built a gazebo. Cara had rented tables and chairs and had decorated them with white linens, bows and fresh day lilies.

Half wishing he could skip the ceremony, he started to turn and go back inside, but Mason strode up to the steps of the gazebo then glanced his way with a smile.

Brody forced one in return. He couldn't let his foul mood ruin his friend's day.

Still, it was all he could do to put on a congenial face as he took a seat in the back row. Weddings made him think of Julie Whitehead, the only girl he'd ever loved.

The girl he'd snuck off to make out with at the rodeo, leaving his brother alone and unprotected.

In the panicked and horrible days after Will had disappeared, he'd lashed out at Julie. He'd blamed her.

But it was really himself he hated.

Dammit, that news report had stirred it all up again, all the haunting memories. He needed to check the database for missing and exploited children, make sure Will's information was still there.

Over the years, he'd focused on making sure local law enforcement agencies as well as state-wide ones didn't give up looking. Even all these years later, he still had hope he'd find his brother.

Although that hope was harder to hold on to every day.

Worse, worry over what his brother had suffered ate at him constantly.

Still, he had to know if he was dead or alive.

SPECIAL AGENT JULIE WHITEHEAD ran her finger over the embossed wedding invitation from Cara Winchester and Mason Blackpaw, then tossed it into the trash. She had worked with Mason on the Slasher case along with Detective Miles McGregor, tracking down a notorious serial killer who'd committed horrific crimes against women. During the case, they'd made friends, but she couldn't bear to attend the couple's wedding—not when it was taking place on the Bucking Bronc Lodge.

Not when Brody Bloodworth would probably attend.

After all, he was the founder of the ranch for troubled boys, a project she whole-heartedly admired, but he was also the man who'd broken her heart. Even after seven years, the thought of seeing him again tore her in knots.

Of course, she hadn't blamed him for hating her after his little brother had disappeared. If it hadn't been for her selfishness, her eagerness to seduce him away from the rodeo, he would have been with Will, and the little boy never would have disappeared.

She'd never forgiven herself for that.

And she'd made it her sole mission in life to see that one day he was found.

The very reason she'd joined the TBI.

Agent Jay Cord, one of the agents who specialized in missing children cases, cursed as he strode over to her desk. "Dammit, did you hear that another little boy went missing?"

Julie's lungs tightened. "Hank Forte. I feel so bad for that family." Memories of the torturous hours after Will's disappearance flashed back. "Any leads?"

"We're still questioning all the workers at the fair, but so far nothing."

She squeezed the stress ball on her desk, knowing the routine all too well. The family was always suspect, a fact that appalled her on their behalf and made her sick at the same time because a large percentage of the time they were guilty.

Next on their suspect list—their friends and relatives. The police and TBI would look into financials, search for motives, the whole time putting out feelers for pedophiles, ex-cons and mental patients. Then the wait for a ransom call. And what to do then?

And if one didn't come…the terrible realization that their child might be dead. "The parents check out?" she asked.

"So far. Both seem devastated. No financial problems. No custody issues. No enemies that they know of."

Julie frowned, thinking of all the cases they'd seen. The first forty-eight hours were crucial. Every second after lessened the chances they would find the child alive.

"I'm headed to Amarillo now," Jay said. "Want to grab a bite of dinner with me on the way? There's a great Italian place I've been wanting to try."

Julie offered him a smile and considered the offer. She knew Jay wanted more from her than friendship or to be coworkers. But even though she liked and admired him, she didn't have it in her heart to get involved with him.

Because your heart belongs to someone else.

No…because her heart had been broken, and she wouldn't take the chance on love again.

Still, maybe she should give him a shot.

Julie stood and reached for her jacket to go with him, but her section chief Lee Hurt, strode in. "Wait a minute, Whitehead. I've got another case for you."

Julie frowned. What could take precedence over looking for Hank Forte?

He strode to her computer, inserted a flash drive, then a second later clicked to open the file. Jay followed, probably wondering if it had to do with the Forte case.

"You've been looking for that kid William Bloodworth for years, haven't you?"

Julie narrowed her eyes. Was he going to reprimand her? "Yes."

"Take a look at this and tell me what you think."

Jay leaned closer and the two of them watched as feed from a security camera filled the screen. Two teenage boys wearing dark hoodies walked into a convenience store, combed the aisles until the few customers inside left, then approached the cashier. Their faces were shrouded in shadows from the hoods, but the taller one held a pistol on the clerk, then demanded all their cash.

"Why are we watching a petty robbery?" Jay asked.

Chief Hurt clicked an icon, and the camera

closed in on the oldest boy. Julie's heart began to pound as his face came into focus.

"Oh, my God," she whispered. "Is it possible?"

Chief Hurt punched another set of keys. "Something about the face seemed familiar so I ran it through our databases, cross-referencing with photos from our missing kids' files and the facial recognition software program that keeps them updated."

Julie's stomach knotted as she watched the computer work its magic. The yearly updates of Will's picture as he'd progressed in age were displayed first, then a comparison shot of the boy at the convenience store and Will's latest sketch.

They were so similar her instincts surged to life.

"I can't believe it," Julie said, stunned. "We've been looking for Will Bloodworth for years, and if this is him, he's surfaced as a criminal?"

"We think it's a local gang," Chief Hurt said. "A group of boys have been robbing stores across Texas."

"Do you think someone bigger is behind it?" Julie asked.

Chief Hurt shrugged. "Maybe. That's what we have to find out."

"I have to tell Will's brother, Brody," Julie said. "He…never gave up hope that Will was alive."

Jay arched a brow. "You've kept in touch?"

Julie shook her head, a pang ripping through

her. "No, but he sends an email periodically to the bureau asking for updates. He's kept his brother's name in front of us to make sure we don't stop looking for him."

Chief Hurt crossed his arms. "Cord, take Special Agent Harmon with you to Amarillo to work on the disappearance of the Forte boy. Whitehead, you're right. Go talk to this kid's brother, tell him what we've discovered."

Emotions pummeled Julie. She'd waited years for this moment, to be able to tell Brody that she'd found his brother. To somehow make right the wrong she'd done years ago.

"Maybe you can convince him to help us find his brother and bring him in," Hurt said.

Julie's chest constricted.

Brody was going to be relieved, even thrilled, to know Will was alive.

But how would he feel when he learned the law wanted him? That once they found him, instead of coming home with him, he would probably go to jail?

BRODY'S CELL PHONE buzzed just as Mason kissed the bride. Laughter and cheers erupted, and the boys from the ranch shifted, anxious for the food. Miles gave his wife a big kiss, which started a chain reaction with all the happy couples in the audience—once again, a reminder that Brody was alone.

Music echoed from the guitar, everyone cheered and clapped, but his phone buzzed again, spoiling the moment. He glanced at the number, ready to let it roll to voice mail. But then he saw the number on the caller ID.

The Texas Bureau of Investigation.

His heart stopped for a moment. He'd memorized that number long ago.

It might not be about Will, he told himself.

Still, hope surfaced. Along with fear.

He knew good and damn well that the call might mean his brother was dead.

The phone buzzed again, and he headed toward the porch as the preacher introduced Mr. and Mrs. Mason Blackpaw and the couple danced down the aisle toward the reception area.

Gritting his teeth, he punched Talk. "Brody Bloodworth speaking."

A breath whispered over the line, making him tense. "Who is this?"

"Brody, it's Julie."

His breath stalled.

"Special Agent Julie Whitehead from the TBI," she continued, her voice slightly shaky.

Jesus, he'd heard she'd gone into law enforcement. Even read that she'd helped Mason and

Miles find the serial killer who'd been cutting up women the last few months.

Picturing her in that role had been hard for him.

"Brody?"

"Yeah, I'm here," he said. "Just shocked to hear from you."

"I'm on my way to the BBL to see you," she said. "It's…about Will."

He closed his eyes, pinched the bridge of his nose to stem the emotions assaulting him. God help him, he had thought he wanted answers.

Now, he wasn't so sure.

Outside, the festivities continued as Mason and Cara cracked open the champagne. Miles McGregor made a toast in celebration of the new life the couple were starting together. They were happy, smiling, looking forward to their future.

Something he hadn't done since that horrible day seven years ago.

Finally, he cleared his throat, willing himself to be strong. He'd waited years for this call; he had to know. "You found him?"

"Yes, we think so," Julie said. "I'll explain when I arrive."

"Explain? What the hell does that mean?" All his pent-up anger, guilt and worry churned through him. "Just tell me, dammit, do you know where he is?"

"Not exactly," Julie said. "Like I said, I'll explain when I get there."

It was on the tip of his tongue to ask the question that had tormented him every night since Will had disappeared, but he couldn't bring himself to.

Not yet.

Julie hung up, and he sat down on the porch swing and knotted his hands into fists and waited. There was no way he could join the celebration right now.

Instead, he watched for Julie's car, knowing she had the answers that he'd told himself he needed to move on with his life.

Only he'd been kidding himself.

The scenarios that screamed through his head did nothing but make him feel sick inside. And the truth, no matter what it was, couldn't be pretty or Julie would have told him over the phone.

He had to brace himself for the worst. Trouble was he didn't know what would be more horrible—finding out his brother was dead, or that he'd been held hostage and abused for years.

JULIE ADMIRED THE sprawling pastures and riding pens as she drove onto the BBL. She'd read about the ranch in the papers and seen pictures of the main house, cabins, stables, camp activities and counseling services offered by the ranch and had been stunned at what Brody had accomplished.

He'd always been a rough, hardworking cowboy and loved riding and roping, but he hadn't grown up wealthy. In fact, his mother had died when he was younger and his father had barely kept their small ranch going.

He'd also blamed Brody when Will had disappeared, destroying his relationship with his son. She wondered if they'd made up before his father had died.

If not, she knew that Brody carried that sting with him.

Maybe it was the reason he'd started the BBL.

She'd also followed the story featuring him as one of the wealthiest ranchers in Texas now. He'd worked his way up on other ranches, made some good investments, and accumulated a fortune.

But instead of letting that wealth go to his head, he'd devoted a huge portion of it to this ranch. He'd also become a role model for troubled boys, which impressed her even more.

She watched several quarter horses running freely in the pasture and smiled. The sight of the animals reminded her of her own dreams when she was young.

She'd wanted to be a vet. Had imagined her and Brody marrying and having a small spread and children. And of course, she would take care of the animals.

A deep throbbing took root in her chest and

wouldn't let go. Those had been a teenager's foolish fantasies.

Again, she glanced at the horses with their beautiful manes dancing in the wind.

Anything to distract her from the task ahead.

And from the idea of seeing Brody again.

God, she had loved him so much.

And he had loved her.

They'd made love and whispered promises to each other in the dark, promises of marriage and family and babies.

Then Will had gone missing and Brody's love for her had turned to hatred.

Gripping the steering wheel tighter, she tried to ignore the pain that memory triggered. She had survived and become a seasoned agent because of it.

Today was about doing her job.

Still, as the big farmhouse came into view with its sweeping trees and the sunset casting golden hues over the land, her heart fluttered crazily.

Brody and some fellow ranchers donated time and money to the project, funding camps, riding lessons and counseling.

There was no doubt in her mind that losing Will had inspired Brody to start the BBL. After all, he'd suffered some hard knocks growing up, but he'd had a tender side, as well, especially for those less fortunate than him.

God knows he'd saved her from the wrath of her uncle a few times.

Shrugging off those memories, as well, she spotted the remnants of the wedding celebration to the right side of the farmhouse. Once long ago when she'd been an innocent girl, she'd fantasized about her own wedding.

But not anymore.

Will's disappearance and the horrific things she'd seen on the job had killed those fantasies.

She struggled to catch her breath. And now she had to destroy Brody's hope that Will would come home safe and happy.

At least he was alive, though. That had to mean something.

She parked, her gaze straying to the front porch of the house and her chest squeezed as she spotted Brody sitting in that porch swing. Seven years had only made him more handsome.

The young boy had become a man, all filled out and muscular. His dark hair was a little longer, nearly brushing his collar, his jawbones just as prominent, his skin a deep bronze from working outside.

He stood as she got out of the car and she swore he'd grown an inch or two in height. She knew every muscle and inch of that skin beneath his chambray shirt, every place that made him moan and sigh with pleasure.

The memory made her yearn to touch him again.

He wore a long duster and a dress shirt indicating he'd been at Mason's wedding when she'd called. But his somber expression told her he held the weight of the world on those broad shoulders.

Then his gaze pinned her with a look of contempt, and she almost wished she'd let another agent handle this job.

But it was her fault Will had gone missing, and she had vowed to herself that one day she'd find him and bring him back to Brody.

Now she knew Will was alive, she had to keep that promise.

No matter how much it cost her.

Chapter Two

Brody had imagined what it would be like to see Julie again, but not like this. Not with her holding the answers that he'd needed for so long.

Still, he couldn't help but look her over. She was more beautiful than he'd remembered. She was slightly slimmer than before, but her figure was still luscious, her hair the color of wheat, her lips pouty, and her eyes the same golden shade of green.

Those eyes had once mesmerized him, seduced him, made him want to give her everything her heart desired. Made him want to save her from that vicious uncle of hers, and promise her the moon.

But instead of the flirty, vibrant glow they had always emanated, instead of the soft innocence he'd known, they radiated with a cold harshness that nearly took his breath.

Because of what she'd seen on the job—or because of him?

The cruel words he'd tossed at her the last time he'd seen her echoed in his head. God, he'd been a bastard. Eaten up with his own guilt and fear.

And he'd taken it all out on her.

"Brody," she said, her voice slightly warbling. "Maybe we should go inside to talk."

The wedding party had left and Brody wasn't sure he wanted to go inside. He needed the fresh air to stem the nausea rolling through him. "Out here is fine."

Her fingers tensed around her shoulder bag, then he noticed it was more of a briefcase than a purse. "I have some things to show you, some photographs," she said indicating the bag. "We really need a place to spread them out."

His gut tightened. Pictures that would tell a story about what had happened to his little brother…

God help him. Did he really want to know?

"I understand this is difficult," Julie said. "Please, Brody, let's go inside and get it over with."

That tone sucked the hope from him. Was she afraid of his reaction?

Afraid of him?

The need to apologize nagged at him, but he couldn't make his voice work. She was right. Prolonging whatever news she'd come to deliver was only putting off the inevitable. Better she tell him then she could leave.

And he could deal with it in his own way.

Resigned, he gestured toward the door, then opened it. She paused to study the foyer when she entered, her gaze sweeping across the hard-wood floors to the winding staircase that led to his master suite and the guest rooms. The downstairs consisted of his own office with other offices available for his partners, and he'd converted the detached garage into a clinic for medical and counseling purposes.

"I heard about the BBL and the wonderful things you're doing here," Julie said. "You should be proud, Brody."

He gave a clipped nod, well aware they were both making polite conversation to avoid the real topic as he led her to his office.

"Do you want coffee?" he asked, still stalling.

She shook her head. "No, thanks." Then she opened her bag and removed a file and laid it on the conference table in the middle of the room.

His stomach twisted, and he leaned his hands on the table and faced her as she sat down. "For God's sake, just tell me, Julie. Is Will dead or is he alive?"

JULIE SIGHED, her heart aching at the pain in Brody's voice. "We think he's alive."

The air left his lungs in a rush. "What do you mean, you *think* he's alive?"

"Sit down, Brody, and I'll explain."

"Sit down?" Brody exploded. "You know how long I've waited to find out what happened to him, and you're dragging it out. Why are you torturing me like this?"

Julie choked back a cry of denial. How could he think she'd be so cruel?

Because he still hates you, still blames you...

She swallowed back her emotions, plastered on her professional mask. She had to pretend like this wasn't personal, treat it like any other case.

"I'm not trying to do that," she finally said. "But it's been seven years, Brody. Children change as they grow up. They...Will won't look exactly the same as he did the last time you saw him."

Brody's face grew pinched. But he sat down in the chair, then raked a hand through his hair. "Okay, tell me what you know. Where is he? What happened to him?"

Julie inhaled a deep breath. "We've used facial recognition software, a program that gives us sketches of what Will might look like as he aged, to keep his file updated."

Brody nodded. "And?"

"We've kept that photo in the national databases, and we got a hit."

"A hit?"

She nodded. "Yes, but we'll have to run DNA to be certain that this teenager is your brother."

Brody clenched his jaw. "Go on."

This was the hard part. "Will showed up in camera feed from a robbery at a convenience store in Amarillo yesterday."

Brody's eyes widened. "A robbery? Who was he with? Was he hurt?"

Julie opened the folder and removed the photos they'd pulled from the camera feed. "He was with another teenager," Julie said. "And no, he wasn't hurt. Will was the one holding a gun on the cashier."

BRODY'S MIND BLURRED for a moment. Did Julie say his brother had held a gun on a cashier? "That can't be right," he said. "Will…wouldn't…"

"Brody," Julie said. "Like I said, we can't be certain it is Will, but it looks like him." She spread another series of shots on the table. "See for yourself."

Brody choked back another protest of denial then leaned forward to study the shots. He wanted to insist that his brother would never rob anyone or use a gun to threaten another person, but it had been seven long years since he'd seen him.

Seven years where Will had been off the grid.

No telling what had happened to him in that time.

"I'm sorry, Brody, I know this isn't what you

wanted to hear," Julie said. "But the good news is that, if this is Will, he's alive."

Her words reverberated in his head. Within a few weeks after Will had gone missing, the police had given up. Since the family hadn't received a ransom note, the authorities had deemed his brother dead.

So they'd stopped looking.

But he'd sworn on his mother's grave that he would never give up.

Julie was right—if this boy was Will, at least he was alive. That meant there was hope he might get him back. But what had happened to him in the meantime?

Would Will even remember him?

Julie shifted, and he jerked his gaze to the photos, determined to ignore the pull of attraction he still felt for her. He was ashamed of the way he'd treated her back then and owed her an apology.

But now wasn't the time. First, he had to find out about his brother.

"What do you think?" Julie asked, all business.

He chewed the inside of his cheek. It was hard to see the teenager's entire face because of that hoodie. A hoodie he'd worn to hide himself from the cameras, meaning he had planned the robbery.

He envisioned his brother the way he was when he'd last seen him. Blondish-brown hair, freckles, crooked teeth, a cowlick that wouldn't quit.

He'd been a pest at times, always following Brody around on the ranch, wanting him to show him riding tricks, spying on him when he'd tried to be alone with Julie.

That last day Brody had been annoyed with him. He'd driven Will to the rodeo, but he and Julie had wanted to slip away and make out, and he'd decided nothing was going to stop him. His old man had always shuffled Will off on him to watch while he boozed it up, and Brody had had enough.

He'd found Will a seat in the stands, thinking he'd stay put until the show was over, then he and Julie had rushed into one of the empty stalls and begun tearing at each other's clothes.

It was the best sex he'd ever had.

And the worst day of his life.

When they'd finally dressed and headed back to the stands, Will had been gone. At first he hadn't panicked. He'd assumed his brother had gone for popcorn or to watch one of the rodeo riders saddle up.

But an hour later total fear had seized him.

That terror had kept him in knots since.

"Brody, what do you think?" Julie asked.

He pushed the haunting memories away so he wouldn't break down in front of Julie. "It looks like him," he said. "But…I can't imagine Will robbing a store. He was always a good kid."

A tense heartbeat passed between them. "We have no idea why Will would rob a store," Julie said. "Or what he's been through the last few years. Someone could have forced him to commit the robbery."

His gaze met hers. She was right.

"There's a gang pulling similar crimes across the state," Julie continued. "It's possible that he was picked up years ago and raised by a family. Maybe for some reason he's gotten in with the wrong crowd and this was some kind of gang initiation."

She was making excuses for him, trying to put the best-case scenario on the situation. It was possible that some loving woman or couple, desperate for a child, had kidnapped Will and raised him as their own.

But they both knew there were other possibilities. The horror stories of pedophiles and kidnappers who abducted children and used them for their own pleasure, who sold them or traded them to other sickos, filled the news. Sex, abuse…the crimes were horrific.

And here in this photo, the teenager, Will, didn't look as if he was being forced to rob the store. It appeared to be a premeditated act.

"If this is him and he's alive, why didn't he try to contact me over the years?" Brody asked.

Another awkward pause, then Julie raked the

pictures back into a stack. "I don't know. It's possible he's suffering from Stockholm syndrome. We'll find out when we catch him."

Brody slanted his eyes toward her, his heart pounding. Of course the police were looking for Will. And when they caught him, they would arrest him.

"Do you have any idea where he is?"

"Not yet," Julie said. "But when we determine a location, we're going to need your help, Brody."

"What do you mean?"

Julie's eyes went cold again. "To bring him in."

Anger heated his blood. He couldn't believe what she was asking of him.

Reeling from the very idea, he paced across the room and stared out the window. Outside, a carriage draped in white lace and ribbons carried Mason and his bride to their cabin for the night. They looked so happy and in love. Soon they'd be leaving for their honeymoon and starting their future together.

A future he'd once wanted with this woman.

But she wasn't the loving, tenderhearted girl he'd known back then. She was a hardened agent who hadn't come here to offer him comfort. No, dammit, she wanted him to set a trap for his brother.

This ranch, the boys, his home…he'd done it all for Will. All in hopes that he'd find him and bring him home.

But Julie wanted him to help send Will to jail instead.

He didn't know if he could do it.

"I understand this is a lot to take in," Julie said, buttoning the navy jacket she wore. Another reminder she was a TBI agent, not here because she cared. "But think about it, Brody."

"What happens if I don't help?"

She dropped her gaze to the file. "Then we go after him by ourselves."

"And if you catch him and he fights back?"

Tension stretched between them for a long second, then she shifted and straightened in the chair. "I'll do everything I can to make sure he's not hurt."

Brody saw red. "Listen here, Julie. My poor little brother has been missing for years, was probably kidnapped, possibly abused and most likely forced to steal, and you cops want to bring him in like he's some hardened criminal. He was a victim, for God's sake."

Julie bit down on her lower lip then stood. "I'm well aware of all that. And like I said, I'll do everything I can to ensure his safety."

Brody hated her cool attitude, the fact that she was here now invading his space, getting his hopes up yet tearing them apart again. Smelling so sweet and feminine and reminding him of all he'd lost.

"Dammit, Julie, when did you get so cold? This may be just a job to you, but it's my brother. If I have to help to make sure he's not hurt and that he gets a fair shake, then I'll cooperate. But my brother is going to receive counseling or whatever help he needs. He is not going to jail."

Julie's eyes flickered with hurt for a brief second before she shut down. But in that second, Brody knew he'd made a terrible mistake. Once again, his emotions had gotten the better of him and he'd lashed out at her.

She snatched up the photos, jammed them in her bag then swung it over her shoulder. "Fine. You can be a jerk to me, but I'm just doing my job. I'll be in touch."

Rage fueled his temper again. She'd be in touch? She sounded like some machine, like there had never been anything personal between them.

Like she'd never let him tear off her clothes and touch her secret, sweet places. Like they'd never made love until both of them were too exhausted to move.

Then she turned and strode out the front door. The sound of it slamming was like a slap to his face.

He needed to apologize.

Thank her for telling him about Will, for not giving up. For personally coming to deliver the news instead of letting some stranger, another agent or cop that he didn't know, do the job.

But by the time he reached the front porch, her car was racing away, disappearing in a cloud of dust.

He leaned against the porch rail and sucked in the fresh air, willing himself to keep it together. Hell, it didn't matter if she was mad at him. He'd lost her a long time ago.

All that mattered was that he find his brother, clear his name and bring him back to the BBL where he belonged.

JULIE TRIED TO control her emotions until she was off the BBL, but the floodgates opened and the tears rained down by the time she left the drive. She'd known coming today wouldn't be easy, that feelings would be raw.

Both his and hers.

But some part of her had hoped that Brody might have forgiven her, that he'd welcome her help.

She swiped at her cheeks, gulping back a sob. Heaven help her, how could she still want him so badly?

Even as she'd told Brody he was a jerk, she knew it wasn't true. He was a good guy. He donated millions to help those troubled kids, had opened up his heart and home to them.

It was just her he hated.

She didn't blame him.

But it still hurt.

You'll get through this just like you have before. Then you'll move onto the next case.

Only Brody had been wrong. Finding Will hadn't simply been a case to her. His disappearance was the reason she'd joined the TBI. The reason she'd devoted her life to tracking down missing kids and putting the bad guys in jail.

It was also the reason she'd never married, the reason she couldn't let Jay into her heart. The reason she'd never been with anyone since Brody.

The reason she never would.

KYLE LET HIMSELF INSIDE the old house, then dumped the cash he'd gotten on the table for his father. The old man wouldn't like the fact that he and RJ had almost gotten caught.

His hand shook as he felt the gun in the pocket of his sweatshirt. Perspiration beaded his neck and hands. He was glad he'd taken the bullets out before the hold-up. He hadn't wanted it to go off and hurt someone.

Even if Father had taught him to kill the enemy, he wasn't a killer.

Footsteps pounded on the steps below, and he stared at the basement door. Locked.

A scream sounded from below. Crying.

The new boy.

Hank, that was his real name. He'd heard the news story on the radio when he'd gone into that store. Hank's parents had been begging people to come forward and help them find their son. They'd acted like they really cared.

But that wasn't what Father said.

The boy cried out again, and Kyle stepped outside, walking far enough away that he couldn't hear the kid's cries. But even as the night sounds of the woods buffeted Hank's pleas to let him go, they resounded in Kyle's head.

He'd spent time in that pit himself. Knew what the darkness felt like. How cold and empty the days were. How terrified it was to be locked up in there alone.

Sometimes he'd been so scared he'd clawed his arms till they bled. He'd tried to remember a time before he'd been brought to Father and enrolled in his army.

But the shadows and night sounds and vile smells in the pit had robbed his mind of those.

He'd been hungry, too. So hungry he'd eaten dirt just to fill his belly. Then he'd been sick and craved water, but Father refused to give him water until he repented and learned to be a good soldier.

Father said it was training, that he had to teach him to be a man.

At first, he'd cried and begged and pleaded for

him to let him out. But that had brought more punishments because men and soldiers didn't cry or beg.

Eventually he'd been so worn down, he'd stopped crying. Stopped begging.

Then Father had let him out.

And he'd believed every word Father said.

Even that his other family hadn't wanted him. That they had sent him to Father to teach him to be strong and to join his army.

But Hank's?

It sounded like his family loved him, that they wanted him back. That they hadn't given him up.

But Father would never let him go now.

And one day Hank would stop crying and learn to do what he had to do to fit in.

Just like he and the others had.

Chapter Three

Julie struggled to pull herself together. Notifying any family member regarding the status of a missing loved one was difficult, but seeing Brody and resurrecting the painful memories of their past was even more difficult than she'd imagined.

Especially because it made her long for the love they had lost.

Not that she had ever seen real love in her life. Her parents had died when she was a baby and her aunt and uncle had taken her in. Her aunt was a sweet, mousy, cowardly woman who'd sat back and allowed her husband to run over her.

Her uncle, a bastard, who had had no business raising a child.

The night Brody had lashed out at her and the following weeks when chaos had descended, the TBI and cops had swarmed, questioning the family, even casting suspicion on Brody's father, had been miserable.

And her uncle had made it worse. He'd found

out she was with Brody and had beaten her and called her a slut.

Two weeks later, she'd left for college, knowing she had to start a new life. She'd sworn never to come back.

Unless it was to bring Brody good news about Will.

It was good news that he was alive, she reminded herself. And when they caught Will, then they could find out the truth about where he'd been all these years.

In spite of the fact that she hadn't seen or heard from her aunt and uncle in years, she found herself driving by their house. The small clapboard structure looked even sadder now. The paint that had once been white had faded to a dingy yellowish brown and was chipped and peeling off. The shutters were rotten, the yard was overgrown, and the flowerbed her aunt had once planted filled with weeds.

Deciding it was time she faced her old demons, she parked, climbed out and walked up to the front door. The screen door was ripped, the winter wind swirling leaves onto the stoop. She knocked, then heard a man's growl from inside and started to turn around and run like she had so many times in high school when her uncle had been on a drunken tear.

But she forced her feet to remain still. She

wasn't a frightened teenager anymore. She was a woman who carried a badge and a gun.

A second later, she heard feet shuffling, then the door creaked open, and her aunt stood on the other side. She looked stoop-shouldered, her hair had gone completely gray, and her eyes were even more lifeless than when she'd lived there seven years ago.

"Aunt Mary," Julie said.

Her aunt's lips parted in shock. "What are you doing here?"

Her uncle grumbled something in the background, then lumbered up behind her aunt. "Who the hell's at the damn door?"

"It's me, Uncle George," Julie said, jutting her chin up in defiance.

He narrowed his eyes, although they were blurred from alcohol. He looked as if he hadn't shaved or showered in weeks.

"It's our Julie," her aunt said. "She's come home."

"No, I haven't," Julie said, hating to dash her aunt's hopes. She'd always been the buffer—rather the punching bag—for her uncle. No doubt after she'd left, he'd turned his wrath on her aunt.

She would always regret leaving her to face that.

"What the hell are you doing here?" her uncle growled.

"I came to talk to Aunt Mary," Julie said, shooting her uncle a glare.

"She doesn't have anything to say to you." Her uncle reached for the door to shut it, but Julie caught it with one hand.

"Wait just a damn minute," Julie said, no longer afraid of her uncle. She simply hated him now. "Aunt Mary, I want you to know that there are better things out there, that not all men are drunks and beat women." Although God knows she'd seen plenty of that on the job. But she used Brody as a model.

"If you ever want to leave this hellhole, you can call me." She shoved her business card in her aunt's hands. "I'll do whatever I can to find you a nice, safe place to live."

"You bitch." Her uncle raised his fist, but Julie pulled her gun and pointed it at him.

"If you lay another hand on her and I find out," Julie said, pinning her uncle with her eyes. "I'll come back, and you'll be sorry."

"Julie dear," her aunt said in that tinny voice that told Julie her aunt had given up a long time ago.

"I mean it," she said. "Uncle George, you may think you can hide what you're doing, but I have my sources now. If you hurt her, I'll find out and I'll be back."

Then she turned around and strode back to her car.

Her uncle's foul mouth spewed obscenities as she climbed into the sedan, but she ignored them and sat for a moment watching the house.

For the first time all day, relief spilled through her and she smiled. Maybe Brody still hated her. Maybe he always would.

But she would love nothing better than to haul her uncle in and put him in jail. She actually hoped he would pull something right now and give her a reason to arrest his sorry ass.

But the house was quiet, and a few minutes later, her aunt walked out onto the front porch and gave her a wave. It was the first time she'd seen her aunt smile like that, and she realized she'd made her point.

So she shifted into gear and drove away.

Her cell phone was buzzing as she pulled onto the main road. She glanced at it, thinking it might be Aunt Mary or Brody, but it was her chief instead.

"What's up?" she asked.

"You know that other kid in the robbery in Amarillo?"

"The boy with the one we think is Will Bloodworth?"

"Yeah. We may have an ID on him."

Julie's heart stuttered. An ID might lead to an address. "And?"

"It's not good," he said. "We think his name is Tray Goodner."

"At least you have a name. Where does he live?"

"That's just it. Tray Goodner disappeared from a neighborhood park five years ago."

A shiver ran up her spine. "You think he and Will were both abducted?"

"It looks that way."

Julie's head spun. "Good God. What if the unsub who'd kidnapped them had also kidnapped Hank Forte?"

THE NEXT TWO days seemed like years to Brody. As he rode to the stables to meet the group of teens he was working with today, he kept replaying the conversation with Julie in his head and berating himself for being so rude.

She was right. He'd been a jerk. But seven years of not knowing what happened to his brother and imagining the worst had stretched his patience to the limits. The pictures of Will robbing that store taunted him.

There had to be a good explanation. Will had been forced to steal to survive.… Maybe he'd been living on the streets and had to join a gang to keep himself safe.…

He checked his phone log for messages, but there was nothing. Dammit, he'd been such a jerk that Julie might have decided not to call him if they located his brother.

The horses kicked up dust as he crossed the pasture, and he steered the quarter horse into the pen. Andrew Cogburn, the twenty-year-old counselor he'd assigned to this trio, threw up a hand in greeting.

The horse they'd just brought in to work with kicked and whinnied, obviously unhappy to be trapped in a pen.

Brody led his horse to another stall, dismounted and patted his side. "Take a break, Chester."

He glanced at the three boys. Fifteen-year-old Hudson "Huddy" Liverby had recently joined the BBL after being sent to juvy for carrying a knife to school. Fourteen-year-old Royce Canton had come with his little brother Tory at the advice of a school counselor who said they were both grieving over their father's recent death. And Seth Tsosis, a twelve-year-old from the reservation, had arrived after his mother had written Brody begging for his help. Seth was having trouble with bullying at school because of his small stature.

"Hi, guys," he said as he approached them.

Huddy scowled, his bad attitude obvious, while Royce seemed interested in watching the stallion bucking in the stall. Seth hugged the edge of the fence as if he was afraid.

"I see you've met Lightning."

"He's mad, ain't he?" Royce said, wide-eyed.

Brody chuckled. "He sure is."

"You ever ride him?" Seth asked.

"Not yet," Brody said. "We just brought him in."

"He looks like he's in jail," Huddy said with a smirk.

"He probably feels that way," Brody said. "He hasn't been broken yet."

"You took him out of the wild?" Royce asked.

Brody shrugged. "Not exactly. But his previous owner wasn't very nice to him."

Seth stiffened. "What'd he do to him?"

"He beat him," Brody said, then gestured toward a couple of scars on the horse's hindquarters. "A friend of mine found him at a rodeo and called me, and we decided to bring him here and see what we could do with him."

Huddy gave him a sour look as if he knew what Brody was trying to do and wasn't buying it. But Brody had learned a lot about kids over the past few years, so he continued.

"There are some other horses on the ranch that are safer and tame, ones you're going to ride while you're here," Brody explained. "So this guy is off-limits for now, got it?"

"I bet I could ride him," Huddy said.

Brody clenched his jaw. "But you won't unless you have my permission," he said firmly. "In fact the first thing you need to learn is a healthy respect for the animals on the ranch. They weigh a lot more than you or I do, and they're powerful creatures. Be good to them and they'll be good to you. But abuse them like the previous owner did and the animal will learn not to trust you."

Royce seemed to be absorbing every word he said, and Seth looked pensive but respectful. Huddy was going to be a problem, but hopefully time would mellow him. A few weeks on the ranch might just turn him into a man.

Andrew motioned toward the pen. "It takes time to break a horse," he said. "But listen, guys, Mr. Bloodworth is the best."

Brody forced a tight smile. "Actually my buddy Johnny Long is the best, but he taught me a lot."

"You know Johnny Long?" Royce asked.

"The rodeo star?" Seth said.

Brody nodded. "Yeah. He's promised to help us with this guy."

"You mean we'll get to meet him?" Huddy asked, losing the belligerence.

Brody held back a smile. Johnny's name always impressed the kids. "You sure will. But Johnny will expect you to learn the basics."

"He's not scared of anything," Seth said with big eyes.

"Actually, that's not true." Brody lowered his voice so as not to make Seth feel as if he was chastising him. "It's okay to be afraid of something bigger and stronger than you are. The key is not to let that fear rule you, and not to allow the animal to know. When an animal senses fear, he'll use it against you just like people do."

Seth looked down at his shoes for a moment as if he was thinking about what he'd said. A minute later he squared his shoulders. "So don't show you're afraid."

"Yes. But that doesn't mean being stupid or jumping into the ring with a big bull or a horse that isn't tame. It means learning how to use your head and handle the animal. To do that, you have to treat them with respect."

Huddy looked sullen again as if he wanted to challenge everything Brody said. But Brody stepped inside the pen, and the horse rose on two legs kicking at him, and the boy's eyes flickered with fear.

"It's okay, Lightning," Brody said gently. He kept his distance, talking softly, as he circled the pen. "The first thing we need to do is to win his trust. And that takes time and patience."

He spent the next half hour talking to the animal and the boys, then led the group into the barn and introduced them to the horses they would learn to ride.

By the time they left the barn and headed to the dining hall, Royce and Seth were chatting excitedly. Huddy had grown quiet, but the tentative way he'd reached out to pat one of the horses indicated he was at least winning his interest in the ranch.

But as Brody watched the boys join the other campers, he looked out at the sea of kids and wondered what Will would think of this place.

For years he'd seen his brother's face on the streets, in stores, every place he went. For a while, he'd attended every rodeo he could find in Texas, hoping his brother would be in the crowd. In fact, a few months ago when Johnny had helped him host a rodeo as a fund-raiser for the ranch, he'd hoped ridiculously that his brother might magically appear in the stands.

But he hadn't.

He shoved his hands in his pockets with a weary sigh. At least he knew now that Will was alive.

And he would do whatever he had to in order to save him.

Even if it meant putting aside his feelings and working with Julie to bring him in.

Two days had passed since Julie had left Brody. Two days of trying to figure out how they could catch Will.

"We've managed to contain the media from showing his photo as of now," Chief Hurt said. "But I don't know how much longer we can hold them off."

"I'm surprised someone didn't capture the robbery on their cell phone and it's not already on YouTube," Julie said.

Agent Jay Cord walked in, looking haggard and worried as hell. "I just came from the Fortes' house. The mother's in bad shape."

As a moment of silence descended, Julie's stomach churned. She wasn't a parent, so she had no idea how it felt to lose the son you'd given birth to, but she did understand the mind-numbing terror and guilt a family felt when a child went missing.

And how devastated she and Brody and Brody's father had been the day they'd lost Will.

"Have the parents, their friends and family all been cleared?" Julie asked.

Jay nodded, then scrubbed a hand over his face. He looked as if he hadn't slept in days. "We got a few tips on that Tip Line, but none of them panned out."

"How could a six-year-old disappear and no one notice it?" Hurt asked.

Julie sighed, the familiar answers traipsing through her head. "It was a busy place, dozens of kids and families around. Kids running off to see the attractions, begging to do the rides, parents trying to keep up." She paused with a huff. "These creeps are pros. They're watching for the perfect opportunity. A balloon floats by and the kid chases it. He sees the ice cream vendor and takes off. His mother, father turn their heads for a second." She snapped her fingers. "That's all it takes."

"Some of them use tricks to lure the kids away from a group," Cord cut in. "A prize, a toy, a puppy. They know how to catch a kid's attention and earn their trust."

"He's right," Julie said. "Just think about it. A man in a uniform, a cop, even a vendor, those people seem safe to children and to the adults around them."

Julie frowned, thinking back to the day Will had disappeared. "You know that could be it. The kidnapper could be someone who worked at the carnival, someone the kids would automatically trust."

"You mean like a vendor?" Cord asked.

"Yes, or someone who got a temporary job working one of the rides or stands. If a man selling cotton candy or giving away balloons came up to Hank, he wouldn't have been scared."

"And the perp might have a van stashed nearby," Agent Cord said, following her line of reasoning.

She removed the photos of Will and the other teenager, Tray, from the file on her desk and spread them out for Jay to look at. "These boys both went missing at different times. Will Bloodworth from a rodeo seven years ago. Tray from a park five years ago."

"You're thinking they're connected?" Cord said.

"It's possible," Julie said. "So maybe we should look back at those sites. The rodeo, the park, the fair. See if there's a connection like an employee, vendor service, even a delivery van."

Jay's face brightened. "Hey, it's more than we had an hour ago and a place to start." He headed to the door. "I'll get right on it. This could be the break we've been looking for."

Julie nodded, her adrenaline pumping. "Tell them to look at all the missing children cases in the past eight years. See how many of them happened at a public venue. There may be more victims attached to this guy."

"You're a genius," Cord said.

Julie shook her head. No, not a genius. Just trying to connect the dots and find Will. He could be only one of a string of children this sicko had abducted over the years.

Just thinking about their families and the pain they'd had to endure made her want to scream in rage.

Agent Hurt's phone buzzed, and he quickly connected the call. "Yes? Right." A slight hesitation, his brows pinched. "Got it. We'll be right there."

He closed his phone then looked at her. "Another robbery in Amarillo. This time there was gunfire. Let's go."

Julie grabbed her bag and rushed out the door

behind her boss, her pulse racing. Normally they wouldn't be involved in a routine robbery case, but since Will's photo had popped up, they had to look at every instance.

By the time they reached the convenience store, two police cars were on the scene, an ambulance was pulling away and spectators had gathered outside.

They jumped out, introduced themselves to the officer in charge, and listened while he filled them in. "Two teenage boys, both wearing black hooded sweatshirts, held up the owner at the gunpoint. Escaped with around five hundred in cash."

Julie watched the ambulance racing away. "Was anyone hurt?"

The officer shrugged. "Nothing serious, but one of the customers tried to play hero and the oldest kid hit him with the butt of the gun."

Julie's chest clenched. If that was Will, then he'd just added assault and battery to the charges against him. The felony charges were racking up.

"Is the man going to be all right?" Chief Hurt asked.

"Yeah," the officer said. "Paramedics took him in for observation."

"Can we talk to the clerk?" Julie asked.

"Sure. We already have officers canvassing the area for witnesses now."

"Good work," Chief Hurt said. "Let me know whatever you find."

They bypassed a couple of kids huddled next to their mother, obviously scared to death, then spotted the clerk talking to another officer as they entered.

"What happened?" Chief Hurt asked.

"Two kids, seemed suspicious, nervous when they came in," the officer said, referring to his notes. "They waited until they thought all the customers had left then pulled a gun and asked for cash."

"How about the man in the ambulance?" Julie asked.

"He was in the john," the clerk said. "Came out and saw what was happening and tried to take the boy with the gun out."

Julie grimaced. The teen would probably claim he was defending himself. But he'd still be charged.

Agent Hurt gestured toward the camera. "Did you record it on film?"

The man nodded, then the officer led them to the camera and flipped it back for them to watch. Julie grimaced as the images spieled onto the screen. Just like the other robberies, the boys had tried to hide their faces, but one angle caught the boy with the gun and it was the same boy in the other photos.

"Did they say anything?" Chief Hurt asked the clerk. "Call each other by name?"

The clerk rubbed a shaky hand over his chin. "Yeah, now that you mention it. The younger kid seemed scared, called the other boy Kyle."

Kyle? Julie gritted her teeth. Either they were wrong about this teen being Will or he was using another name.

Her cell phone buzzed, and she checked the number. Brody.

She nudged Chief Hurt. "Excuse me, I'll be right back." Her finger itching to answer the call, she stepped aside.

"Julie, it's Brody." His voice resonated with worry. "I just saw the news report about that other robbery. Was it Will?"

Julie clenched the phone. "It is the same two teenagers in the other robbery," she said. "But I told you we can't be sure until we get DNA."

"I know that," he said. "But I saw the picture on TV."

Julie hissed. This couldn't be good.

"Brody, we're at the scene interviewing the cashier now. She said the younger boy called the other one Kyle, not Will."

A tense second passed. "So, he could have assumed another name?"

"Yes. It's not uncommon for kidnappers to do

that to their victims." She hesitated. "I just wanted to warn you."

"Warn me what?" Brody asked. "That whoever kidnapped him may have made him change his name?"

"Yes," Julie said. "There's no telling what Will has been through in the past seven years. When you see him, you have to remember that."

She shuddered at the thought as a dozen different scenarios raced through her head. None of which she wanted to share with Brody.

BRODY'S LUNGS tightened as he realized the implications of what she'd said. Even if this was Will, he might not want to come home.

Hell, Will might not remember him at all.

"I've seen the stories about other abductions," Brody said. "Where some kidnappers brainwash their captives, force them to forget their pasts. And in some cases, the kidnapper actually made them believe they were someone else."

Her throat clogged with emotions. "That's true," Julie said. "So just be prepared."

No…Brody didn't believe it. Will would remember him. And he'd want to come back home.

"You asked for my help before," Brody said. "Just tell me what you need, Julie. I'll do whatever it takes to bring Will in."

It was the only way to find out the truth about what had happened and save his little brother.

But would Will come with him when he did?

KYLE USHERED RJ into the old house. But as soon as he stepped inside, Father grabbed him and gave him a hard knock across the face. He staggered back, tasting blood, then his father cursed as he lunged for him again.

"You stupid little jerk, your face is all over TV."

Kyle's stomach lurched as he remembered what had happened to the last kid who'd gotten caught.

They had all paid for it.

And the boy—he'd ended up dead.

Of course his father had told him the boy had run off.

But he'd lied.

Kyle had seen Father bury him in the backyard that night. He'd seen another grave there, too. He didn't know who was in it.

But Father would bury him back there, too, if he didn't behave.

Chapter Four

Brody had never been to the TBI office, and was surprised at the interesting architecture and modern touches in the building's design.

The inside looked spotless, with office spaces on various floors. But even though the building was sleekly designed, an ugliness permeated the rooms.

Bulletin boards were clogged with photos of various ongoing cases. Most of the agents wore dark suits and even darker expressions that made him wonder why Julie chose to stay in this world.

As a teenager, she'd loved animals and had worked on a ranch during the summers, grooming and exercising horses, and giving riding lessons to children. She'd also trailed after the local veterinarian and had talked about attending vet school.

But sometime after they'd parted she'd changed her mind.

It had to do with Will, he realized as the recep-

tionist led him into the conference room where
Julie sat with two other agents, both of whom were
studying a wall of mug shots of young boys. The
sight made his skin crawl.

And made him realize what he'd done to Julie
by blaming her for his brother's disappearance.
Heaping that guilt on her had been unfair, but
she'd obviously used it to inspire her to work in
law enforcement just as he'd used his own guilt
to inspire the BBL.

"Special Agent Whitehead," the receptionist
said. "Mr. Bloodworth is here."

Julie glanced up, her face drawn, and emotions
clogged his throat. God, he'd been wrong to lash
out at her. To lay guilt on her for his wrongdoing.

She should have been taking care of animals,
living on the ranch, not here in this world of con-
stant misery and crime.

"Come in, Brody," Julie said, gesturing for him
to take the chair beside her. "We're discussing
the case."

So his brother was just a case to them. But not
to Julie. Now he saw the pain in her eyes. Pain he
had put there by his own anger and guilt.

"This is Section Chief Hurt and Special Agent
Cord," Julie said, indicating the two men.

"Do you have something new on my brother?"
Brody asked after they shook hands.

"We have a theory." Chief Hurt pointed to the

photos of the other missing boys. Brody took a visual sweep and counted a total of ten.

"You think these missing boys may have been abducted by the same person who kidnapped Will?" Brody asked.

"We don't know, but it's possible. We have agents reviewing each of the boys' cases and talking with their families. The disappearances started about twenty years ago."

"Which means some of the children would be young men in their early twenties now," Julie interjected. "That is, if they're still alive."

Brody's blood ran cold. "You think he keeps them for a while, then kills them?"

Julie shrugged. "At this point we can't say. But the fact that this boy Kyle, if he is Will, is still alive, gives us hope that some of the victims are still alive, as well."

"How could this guy get away with this crime for twenty years?" Brody asked.

"It's possible that the kidnapper keeps his victims locked up most of the time. He lives off the grid, maintains a low profile, possibly holds a menial job, if he has one, so he doesn't raise suspicion."

Brody tried not to think about where the man kept the boys. Or what he might do to them in the dark.

"But I don't understand." Brody scrubbed a

hand over his chin. "Those teenagers walked into that convenience store on their own. Why don't they tell someone what's going on and ask for help?"

Julie exchanged concerned looks with the other agents.

"Look, don't hold back," Brody said. "I can handle the truth. All I want is a chance to try and get my brother back."

"There are different possibilities," Julie said. "Sometimes victims fall prey to Stockholm syndrome."

"Other times the kidnapper has threatened the victim, his family, or a loved one. The kidnapper keeps him isolated and terrorizes his victim, even abuses him or her. When he feels like he has total control, that he has successfully brainwashed the victim, he may give him the chance to prove himself by taking him out in public."

"If this unsub, unknown subject, is now in his forties, he may not be employed anymore. Either he's out of work for health reasons or he came close to getting caught or noticed, and he had to lay low. That may be the reason he's forcing the older kids to bring in money by stealing," Agent Cord said.

Brody noticed the little boy Hank's photo on the wall. "You think that child was taken by him, too?"

Julie bit her lip. "We're not certain, but it's possible. Each of these children disappeared from a public venue like a carnival, public park, county fair, a rodeo—" She paused and met his gaze. "He may work at one of these venues. He's friendly, fits in, doesn't look like a criminal. That's how he gets close to the kids."

"So you can track him down that way?" Brody asked.

"That's what we're working on," Chief Hurt said.

Dammit, they needed to work faster.

Julie stood then went to the board and gestured toward a map with pushpins stuck in various areas. "The convenience store robberies over the past few months also coincide with areas where children went missing, which also makes us believe they're connected. Hopefully if we find this gang of robbers, it will lead us to other missing children."

"How can I help?" Brody asked. "Do you want me to go on TV and make a plea for Will to come forward?"

"No," Julie said, her eyes darkening with worry. "That might endanger Will and Tray, the boy with him. We don't want to tip this guy off that we're getting close to uncovering his identity."

"*Are* you getting close?" Brody asked, his patience on thin ice.

Julie tensed, one hand worrying her jacket buttons. "We think so," Julie said. "In fact, we've narrowed down stores we suspect may be targeted next and are placing undercover officers on surveillance duty to monitor them."

Brody's heart pounded as he imagined Julie in a car at night watching for a group of robbers to attack a store at gunpoint.

Cold fear knotted his stomach as he realized the danger she was putting herself in.

"Are you working these stakeouts?" he asked.

Julie's gaze met his. "That's my job."

"Then I'm going with you."

Chief Hurt and Agent Cord mumbled disagreement, but Brody stood his ground. "You have to let me do this. If you catch Will in the act, I may be the only one who can reach him." He walked over and pointed to the board of boys. "You said yourself that finding him may lead to these other victims. You can't afford not to let me go."

JULIE KNEW Brody was right. But that didn't mean she had to like it. This case was difficult enough for her—the guilt kept sneaking up on her at the oddest times and had kept her awake the last few nights—but the thought of working alongside Brody made her even more jittery.

Just breathing in the same air as Brody made her want him again.

"You know I'm right," Brody said in that gruff voice that twisted her insides.

"He has a point," Chief Hurt said.

Julie fidgeted. "I know, but it could be dangerous."

Brody glared at her. "It's not dangerous for you?"

He was practically daring her to admit that she was scared. "It's my job," Julie said, knowing Brody was one of those macho cowboys who thought he was tougher and rougher than any woman ever could be.

Agent Cord chuckled. "Hey, how about a truce, you two? The most important thing here is to stop this gang and find out who's behind it. That is, unless it's just a group of street thugs led by the older boy Kyle."

"My brother is not a street thug," Brody said, obviously irritated. "However he's involved in this, there's a story behind it, and it started seven years ago when he was abducted."

"You still don't know for certain that he was abducted," Agent Cord said, raising an eyebrow. "He could have run away."

"That's ridiculous, Will would never have done that. He was a happy, well-adjusted kid back then." Brody's gaze veered to the wall. "And if the cops had done their jobs, Will could have been saved, and so could these others."

"That's not fair, Brody," Julie cut in, her look tortured.

Chief Hurt threw up his hands. "Casting blame is not helpful." He pivoted toward Brody, and crossed his arms. "I agree that if the boy with the gun is your brother, then you might be able to reach him. But remember, Brody, you are not an official law officer. You will stay behind the scenes and take orders from Agent Whitehead."

Julie bit back a smile at the uncomfortable look on Brody's face. He was accustomed to being in charge. Taking orders from her would probably make him change his mind.

But he cast her a look, his jaw tightening. "I'll do anything to get my brother back, even if it means taking orders from her."

Julie frowned, but Chief Hurt took the lead, assigning each of them different territories to cover.

"I have a friend in law enforcement who might be able to assist," Brody said. "Detective Miles McGregor. He worked the Slasher case a few months ago."

"Sure, I know him," Chief Hurt said. "I'll call him and catch him up to speed."

The meeting was dismissed, and Julie summoned her professional demeanor, knowing she couldn't allow herself to feel anything for Brody now.

He was a case, an unfinished one, but one that she needed to close.

And that was all he could ever be.

"So how do we do this?" Brody asked as he followed Julie through the hall and outside to her dark sedan.

"We pick up coffee, find a place to park, look inconspicuous and wait."

Brody caught her arm as they made it to the car. "I… Thanks for letting me come along." He wanted to say so much more. Tell her she didn't have to put herself in danger to save strangers. That she should be taking care of sick animals, not carrying a gun and putting herself in the line of fire.

But she shrugged off his touch as if she was annoyed to have him along, then climbed in the car and started the engine. By the time he fastened his seat belt she'd pulled into traffic, a thick silence falling between them.

He couldn't stand the quiet. Couldn't stand knowing that she rode these streets alone looking for criminals.

That she could get herself killed.

Then he reminded himself that he hadn't seen her in seven years. She might be involved with someone else now, might even be married.

A quick check to her ring finger though and he didn't spot a ring.

Julie pulled through a doughnut shop, ordered two coffees and an assortment of doughnuts, then handed him his coffee. For the next two hours, they staked out a convenience store. The conversation was stilted, the air filed with tension every time they watched someone enter the store.

A black teen wearing a hoodie entered, a white kid beside him, and Brody sat up straighter, watching through Julie's extra set of binoculars as they combed through the store.

"Think they're canvassing it?" he finally asked.

Julie sighed. "Maybe."

The boys approached an older man, passed him a few bucks, then the guy bought a six-pack of beer, and carried it outside. The kids bought a bag of chips and pretzels, then met the older guy on the curb and raced off with the beer.

"You going to bust them?" Brody asked.

Julie shook her head. "Not worth it. Besides we can't draw attention to the fact that we're here."

Right. They were waiting for the bigger fish.

Nerves climbed his neck. "How do you do this all the time?" he asked.

"This is not all I do," she said, her eyes still trained on the store.

He'd seen enough TV crime shows to know

that was true. But he didn't like the images that flashed through his head.

Julie's cell phone buzzed, and she grabbed it, speaking low into the mouthpiece. "Right. We'll be right there."

"What?" Brody asked as she cut the connection, then swung the car around and headed south.

"They hit a store a couple of blocks from here. Hang on." She pressed the accelerator, and Brody's pulse clamored as she sped around traffic. Was this it?

After all these years, was he finally going to see his brother again?

"It's not good," Julie said as she swung around the corner, tires squealing. "One of the locals moved too soon and freaked the boys. The younger one, Tray, escaped, but Kyle has a hostage."

Brody choked back an obscenity, then Julie threw the car up on the curb and reached for her gun.

His heart hammered double time as he climbed out with her. "Julie?"

Her gaze met his, her beautiful eyes tortured but focused. "I promise you, Brody, I'll do everything I can to make sure Will's not hurt."

He had trusted her with his heart years ago, trusted in their love. But this was his brother's life.

He didn't want her getting hurt, either.

"Brody, trust me," she whispered in a raw voice.

Pain wrenched through him, but he gave a clipped nod, then they both climbed out. The two officers on the scene, Officers Damon Lewis and Jamie Fenton, introduced themselves.

"We saw the robbery in progress and started to go in, but the other kid must have spotted us and told the boy with the gun. Suddenly all hell broke loose," Officer Fenton said.

"How many are inside?" Julie asked.

"Just the perp and the cashier," Officer Lewis supplied. "A young girl about the kids' age. She's scared out of her mind."

Two more police cars raced up, lights flashing, the cops jumping out, taking cover behind the car where Fenton and his partner had gathered.

"We need a hostage negotiator," Officer Lewis said.

Officer Fenton nodded. "And the SWAT team. Get the captain on it ASAP."

"Wait a minute," Julie said. "Let me see if I can talk to the kid and diffuse the situation."

Brody's chest was about to explode with fear. "No, Julie, let me. If this is Will, maybe he'll recognize my voice."

Julie's hand brushed over the weapon strapped in her holster. "And if it's not?"

Brody gave her a pleading look. "I know what I'm doing, Julie. I work with scared kids, teenagers that have been in trouble with the law, on the BBL everyday. Let me give it a shot."

Julie slanted him a warning look. "Don't take any chances, Brody. Just talk." She poked him in the chest, her voice edged with worry. "Even if he is Will, we don't know his state of mind or what drove him to this point. What we do know is that he's desperate, scared and armed."

Brody drew a deep breath. He knew all that, but he didn't care.

Besides, if he didn't do something, these cops might get cocky or spooked and open fire or swarm the place.

Then his little brother might get killed.

And he would take a bullet himself before he allowed that to happen.

Chapter Five

Brody watched the police and agents huddle, with a sickening knot in his stomach. They had cordoned off the area, and stationed cars to keep anyone else from pulling into the parking lot. Another team had gone in search of the second boy who'd run from the scene.

It also looked as if the TBI agent, Hurt, was having a heated discussion with the officer in charge about how to handle the situation and who should take the lead.

Chief Hurt must have won because he grabbed the bullhorn. "Order all your men to stand down," he said. "No one fires unless I give the word."

"Yes, sir," the officer growled.

"You're surrounded by the police," Chief Hurt said into a bullhorn. "We know your name is Kyle and that you're in a bad spot. You just wanted some money tonight, not to hurt anyone."

Brody strained to see inside the convenience

store. There were two figures near the door, the boy and the girl.

"Get out of here," Kyle yelled. "Let me go and the girl won't get hurt."

Brody saw the girl's terrified expression and heard the desperation in Kyle's voice. He tried to remember the sound of Will's voice to compare it to the young man, but Will hadn't even reached adolescence when he'd disappeared. His voice would have changed, grown deeper, more manly.

"You're not leaving here," Chief Hurt said. "That's a given. So release the girl, and we can make some kind of deal."

"I can't go to jail," Kyle shouted. "I can't."

The two officers on the end looked restless. "It's time for SWAT," one of them muttered.

"I can try to go in the back door," the other officer suggested.

Chief Hurt glared at them. "No. We can't risk a hostage being injured."

Brody sensed the situation spiraling out of control. A news van rolled up, a cameraman and reporter climbing out.

"This is Wanda Thorn coming to you live. We're at the scene of a hostage situation."

"Make that camera disappear," Kyle yelled.

Julie motioned toward Chief Hurt. "I'll handle it." She headed over to talk to the reporter, then

Brody strode toward the agent. If he left it up to them, they'd storm in and kill his brother. Rather, Kyle.

He had to do something.

"Let me talk to him."

Chief Hurt glanced at him with narrowed eyes then gave a clipped nod, and Brody grabbed the bullhorn.

"Will, I know you haven't seen me in a long time, but it's me, Brody, your brother."

He hesitated, hoping for a response. Someone moved inside, then the two figures appeared at the front door. The glass was foggy though, and he could only make out part of the boy's head behind the girl.

"Please help me," she cried.

"Will, please," Brody said. "You don't want to hurt that girl. Just put down the gun."

"My name is not Will," the boy yelled. "Now get out of here so I can leave, and the girl will be fine."

Chief Hurt shot him a concerned look. "Like we said, he may not remember you."

"Okay, Kyle," Brody said. "I'm sorry, I was confused. I lost my brother a long time ago. He was kidnapped when he was ten, and I've been looking for him ever since."

"Well, I'm not your brother," Kyle shouted.

"All right, it's just that you remind me of him."

Julie slipped up behind him, and squeezed his arm. "He was a good kid, and I'm sure you are, too," Brody continued. "But you're in a bad spot right now. Listen, I know this agent here, Julie Whitehead. She'll give you a fair shake if you cooperate."

"Then tell her to clear out the damn cops."

"I'm trying to get them to back down," Brody said. "And they have orders not to shoot. But you have to let the girl go, Kyle. If you hurt her, I won't be able to help you."

The officers shifted, one moving his gun so it was trained on the door. Nerves clawed at Brody. He lowered his voice to a soft murmur so only Julie could hear, "Julie, that cop looks trigger-happy."

Julie motioned toward ChiefHurt, and he spoke in a low voice into the mike to the officer, hopefully warning him to back down.

Then Brody had an idea. He'd worked with troubled kids long enough to know that this boy was scared. He'd been backed into a corner, and he didn't know what to do or how to get out of the situation.

Brody had to offer him a way out.

"I'm coming in," he said, slowly starting toward the store. "Send the girl out and you can take me as a hostage instead."

"Brody, stop." Julie caught his arm, but he shook off her concern.

"I have to do something," Brody said. "I can't let them hurt Will."

Julie hissed a protest as he strode forward. "Kyle, did you hear me?"

"Stay back," Kyle shouted.

"I'm not going to do that," Brody said. "I won't leave you here like this. I'm coming in so we can solve this problem together."

"How do I know you don't have a gun?" Kyle asked.

Brody shrugged out of his jacket, then patted himself, turning around in a circle to give the teenager a clear view. "See, no gun. I just don't want to see you or the girl hurt."

Tension thrummed through the air as he took another step closer. He felt Julie's eyes on him, the other cops bracing for gunfire, but he didn't stop.

Maybe this teenager wasn't Will. But he needed help, and Brody didn't intend to turn back now. "Open the door," he said as he approached it. "Send her out and I'm all yours."

The door squeaked open, the girl's tear-streaked eyes meeting his.

"Come on," he said as he motioned her forward. "I'm yours, Kyle, just let her walk away."

The girl suddenly stumbled forward, and Brody grabbed her arm and pulled her behind him. A second later, her footsteps pounded behind him, but he kept his gaze fixed on the boy. In his peripheral vision, he saw Chief Hurt rush forward, grab the girl and pull her to safety. The camera flashed, the reporter speaking into the mike.

"The female hostage has just been released, but this is not over yet, folks."

Brody's heart raced as he struggled for a way to reach the boy. He searched for his brother somewhere in the kid. Kyle had brown eyes like Will, that cleft in his chin. This boy had scars though, one above his eye, more on his arms.

He gritted his teeth. How many bruises and scars were hidden? And who had put the injuries there?

"Just stay calm," he said in a low voice. "I run a ranch for kids near here," Brody said. "I think you'd like it. Do you know how to ride?"

Sweat beaded on the boy's face, his eyes darting toward the cops in a panicked haze. "The only thing I want to do is ride out of here."

Kyle raised his gun and aimed it at him, then motioned for him to turn around. "You have a car here?"

"Yes." He'd use Julie's car if he needed to.

"Let's go."

"Sure thing," Brody said.

He turned and allowed Kyle to use him as a shield as he started toward the sedan.

But Chief Hurt stepped from behind his dark sedan. "Hold it right there."

Julie inched toward them. "Kyle, let me help you," Julie said gently. "We'll work out some kind of deal."

"I told you I'm not going to jail." Kyle pressed the gun into Brody's back, and Brody tensed.

A second later, the sound of a gun being cocked split the air, then a shot rang out.

Brody jerked around to push Kyle out of the way. At the same time, Julie rushed forward, throwing herself between the shooter and him. The bullet whizzed by her head, then she hit the dirt.

Brody's heart stalled in his chest. Dear God, had Julie been shot?

JULIE ROLLED IN the dirt, braced to shoot the stupid cop who'd opened fire. But everything happened too fast. Chief Hurt and the other officer both dove at Kyle and Brody. Brody spun around and tried to block them from reaching Kyle, but Hurt was too fast and knocked the gun from the boy's hand while the officer aimed his weapon at the boy's head.

"Move and it's all over," the officer growled.

"Dammit," Brody snarled. "Don't shoot him, he's just a kid."

"Hold your fire," Chief Hurt said to the officer. Then he snapped handcuffs on Kyle.

The boy spat a belligerent string of words at Hurt, jerking in protest as the agent grabbed his arm.

"Keep calm," Brody said, holding out a hand toward Kyle. "We'll figure this out together, I promise you're not alone."

Chief Hurt shoved Kyle toward his car, and Julie pushed up from the ground, swiping the dirt off her clothes. She rushed toward Brody. She had to make sure he was okay.

But when she touched his arm to comfort him, Brody stormed at her. "What the hell were you doing?"

Julie gasped at the vehemence in his tone. "I was trying to save your sorry butt," she hissed.

He took her arm, then ran his eyes over her from head to toe. "You almost got yourself shot."

"I was just doing my job," she said, anger mounting. For God's sake, she'd had to battle enough male prejudice to earn her ranking as an agent. She hadn't expected it from Brody.

Brody's erratic breathing echoed in the air as he tilted her face up toward him. "Are you hurt?"

His trembling voice touched emotions deep inside her, and she realized he was reacting more out of fear than male prejudice.

Still, she couldn't cut him any slack. Especially here in front of her superior.

"I'm fine, Brody. I was trying to make sure the boy wasn't hurt."

His gaze latched onto hers for a long moment, the fear and pain in his expression wrenching her heart. He started to speak, but the commotion around them suddenly went crazy as the reporter raced toward Kyle and the cameraman flashed more pictures.

Julie pulled away from Brody and strode toward the woman. "That's enough."

The woman simply beamed at her. "You're with the TBI, aren't you, ma'am? Would you give us a statement?"

Julie frowned at her, then cleared her throat. "I'm sorry, but we can't comment on the arrest at this moment due to an ongoing investigation. Thank you."

Chief Hurt stood beside Kyle at his car. The blue lights twirled in the darkness, the other officers who'd gathered mumbling and working to control the spectators.

Julie hadn't realized how much the crowd had grown.

Then her gaze caught Kyle's face in the twirling lights. The bruises on the boy looked stark, some old, some fresh. Kyle deftly turned his head away from the cameras to avoid being photographed.

Had his kidnapper seen his photo on screen before? Had that triggered the beating that left those marks?

Was the bastard watching now?

BRODY HATED THE FEAR that had nearly choked him when Julie had hit the dirt. He'd also been terrified that Will—Kyle—would get shot, and he'd had to protect him.

Even if it turned out Kyle wasn't Will, the teenager needed help. The bruises on his face and arms indicated he'd been severely abused.

The question was—who was abusing him? And would the boy give up his or her name?

He'd worked with enough troubled kids to know that ratting out their abuser was difficult. Both fear and the desperate need for love from the very person mistreating them drove the victim to keep silent.

"They're going to take Kyle to booking at the local police station," Julie said. "Chief Hurt and I will question him there."

"You know he's being beaten," Brody said in a strained voice.

Julie's expression turned grim. "Yeah, I saw the bruises." She tucked her weapon back in her holster, and he frowned. He didn't want her working this job, putting her life on the line.

"I assume you want to be there," Julie said,

cutting her gaze toward Chief Hurt's sedan as he started it up.

Brody's heart hammered as he caught sight of the boy. Kyle was slumped over in the backseat, hiding his face from the cameras and spectators.

"Yes, let's go." The reporter suddenly made a beeline for him, but he and Julie jogged to her car and jumped inside, dodging her attack.

Brody tried to wrangle his emotions under control as Julie drove, but the scene with the police and the boy and Julie kept tormenting him. He wanted to tell Julie to quit her job.

But he had no right.

After all, hadn't he driven her to it by his cruel accusations after Will went missing?

God, he had to fix things with her, to apologize.

"Just so you know what's going to happen," Julie said, cutting off his thoughts. "He will be booked for armed robbery, and endangering another life. At his age, the DA can push for him to be tried as an adult."

Brody pulled a hand down his chin. "What about the fact that he's being abused? That he may be my brother, may have been kidnapped and forced to rob that store?"

Julie reached out and laid a hand over his. "Don't worry, Brody. I'll find out who he really is and what's going on with him. And if he is Will and has been forced to steal, the court will hear that, too."

Brody relaxed slightly, his hand aching to curl into Julie's and latch onto her. She was so strong and gutsy that it made him realize how much she'd changed.

That she'd toughened up since he'd last known her.

Of course she'd had to in order to do her job.

"Thank you," Brody said. "I…even if he isn't Will, I want to help him."

Julie glanced at him as she followed the squad car and Chief Hurt toward the jail. "You're a good man, Brody. I admire what you've done at the BBL."

His throat ached, the old feelings he'd had for her burning in his chest.

"I guess we've both tried to help other kids to make up for what happened to Will."

She tensed, but he gripped her hand and squeezed it. "I'm sorry, Julie. I…was wrong to blame you back then."

"No, you were right," she said, self-derision lacing her voice as she cast her eyes back on the road. "If I hadn't begged you to go to the barn with me that day, you would have been with Will and he never would have disappeared."

"That's probably true," Brody said. "But it wasn't your fault. I wanted to go to the barn with you," he admitted. "Hell, that's all I'd thought about for days. Weeks even." His voice cracked. "As much as I hate to admit it, I was tired of always watching out for him." Shame filled him. "That's why I lashed out at you. I was really angry with myself."

Julie released a slow breath. "You were a good brother to Will," she said softly. "He adored you, and I know how much you loved him, Brody. But you were young. We both were, just doing what teenagers do."

Brody nodded. "I've told myself that a hundred times, but it doesn't make the guilt go away."

Another pained second passed. "I've worked a couple of other kidnappings/missing children cases," Julie said. "Every parent and sibling, even the friends of the victim, always blame themselves. But the truth is that predators are everywhere. Sometimes it's a crime of opportunity. They see a kid off by themselves and abduct the child. Sometimes, that person has been stalking the child for a while just waiting on the opportunity to arise to snatch him without anyone noticing."

"My father went through all that with the cops back then," Brody said. "The police questioned all the employees at the rodeo, and as many spectators as they could. Some had already left by the time we realized Will was missing."

"I know, I've studied the files."

Brody's gaze latched with hers. "You have?"

Julie nodded, then swung the car into the parking lot of the jail. "But if this case is connected to the Forte boy's disappearance, and to those others cases on the wall, then maybe Kyle can lead us to this bastard and we can save the victims he has."

Brody nodded, although Kyle's face flashed in his mind.

If Kyle was Will and he'd been abused to the point of not recognizing him or remembering his own name, would he give up his abductor's name?

Would Brody ever get his brother back?

KYLE KEPT HIS head low as the policeman dragged him from the back of the car and shoved him into the police station.

Dammit to hell. The TBI had him.

A string of expletives rolled through his head. What was going to happen now?

He wasn't worried about himself.

But the others…

They were counting on him.

Father was already pissed that his face had shown up on the screen. He didn't want any suspicion coming back to him. He'd pounded that in him over and over the night that news story had aired.

Today had been his chance to redeem himself.

And he'd failed.

The cop pushed him toward booking where they took his fingerprints. Kyle began to sweat. They would hammer him with questions and want to know about the other kid who'd been with him. Want to know if anyone else was involved.

Want to know about his parents and where he lived.

He had to keep his mouth shut.

Father would kill him if he talked.

No…worse. He'd make the others suffer and force him to watch.

Then he'd bury him like he had the other two boys.

Chapter Six

Brody felt helpless as they followed the police car from the local station to the TBI headquarters in San Antonio. Will—Kyle—had been processed by the police, but Julie had insisted he be transported immediately to the state's federal facility, claiming jurisdiction over the locals, which seemed to piss them off.

But she'd held her ground, using the fact that Will might be the victim of a serial kidnapper as leverage.

"What do you think?" Julie asked as they stepped into their break room to get a cop of coffee while Agent Cord escorted the boy to an interrogation room.

"I think he's Will," Brody said, going with his gut. "But...dammit, Julie, how can I not know for sure?"

Julie stirred sweetener into her coffee and gave him a sympathetic look. "It's been seven years," she said softly. "Will went missing before he hit puberty so his body and voice changed."

"But those eyes…" Brody let the sentence trail off as he remembered the distant look on the teenager's face. Sure, his eyes were brown like Will's, and he had a cowlick, but Will had always had a mischievous light in his eyes that gave him life.

This boy's eyes looked troubled, cold, flat as if he'd seen the dark side of life and had given up on anything better.

He'd seen that same look in a few of the kids who came to the BBL. Sometimes he'd helped them turn their lives around, but he'd also failed with two of the older kids. Life had taught them to be hard, to use force to survive, and anger was so ingrained in them that it would take years of counseling to temper it.

"We'll push him to find out his real name," Julie said. "But I've requested DNA testing to confirm his identity."

"I still think I could reach him," Brody said. "That if I talk to him, remind him of how we grew up, things we did together, that he'll remember me."

Julie squeezed his arm. "I know you're anxious to be with him, Brody, but first let me do my job. There's more at stake here than just his identity."

Brody's jaw tightened. "You mean the armed robberies?"

"Yes, that and the fact that his kidnapper may

have abducted other boys, and he might lead us to them."

He wanted to argue that all he cared about was Will.

But an image of the parents of the Forte boy flashed in his head, and he bit his tongue. He knew the pain of wondering, not knowing, missing a loved one.

He'd never wish that torture on anyone else.

"Come on," Julie said. "Do you want to watch the interrogation?"

Brody swallowed hard. He had to observe in case Kyle gave himself away in his mannerisms, his body language, or even something small he said.

Then he would know who the boy really was.

That would be the first step in helping him.

Still, he braced himself as he followed Julie to an adjoining room with a one-way mirror. The fact that Kyle had bruises told him his story wasn't going to be pretty.

He just wondered how ugly it would get.

"ARE YOU sure you're up to this, Brody?" Julie asked. "Watching us interrogate Kyle may be difficult. We have to ask him some hard questions. And if he isn't cooperative, we'll have to push."

A muscle jumped in Brody's cheek, his look

glazed with pain and resignation. "I want the truth," he said. "Do what you have to do."

Julie's gaze met his for a heartbeat, then she gave a small nod. "Just remember that he's been traumatized, so uncovering that truth may take time."

"I know. I've waited seven years. At least if he's alive, I have hope again."

Julie's heart ached for him. She wanted to drag him into a hug and comfort him like she would have done years ago, but touching him made her want more.

And she couldn't afford to travel down that road again.

"I'll be back in a few minutes," she said. "Hang in there."

He mumbled that he would, then crossed his arms and faced the window, and Julie left the room.

But worry seized her insides. She hoped she was doing the right thing by allowing Brody to watch. But she hoped Kyle might give some clue that Brody would pick up on to confirm that he was Will.

Normally DNA testing took time, but she'd requested a rush on it, reasoning that this unsub registered on the MOST WANTED list, so she hoped to have the results soon.

If their theory was right and Kyle had been abducted by the same man who'd kidnapped little Hank Forte, and the unsub realized Kyle had been caught, he might panic, take the boys and run.

Then they might lose any link to him.

God knows, the bastard had been living under the radar for years and getting away with his crimes.

She wanted to put him away this time and make him pay for what he'd done to those children and their families.

BRODY WATCHED JULIE enter the interrogation room, Agent Cord behind her. He had to trust her to do the right thing with his brother.

She was a trained agent.

But she'd also known Will as a child. Had played games with him, shared picnics, even helped him with homework. He remembered them making PB and Js with honey and wading in the creek. Questioning Kyle had to be hard for her, too.

If this kid was Will, would he recognize her? She'd been in their house a lot that last year— maybe he would remember her. If so, somehow that might make the interrogation easier for him to endure.

Forcing himself to focus, he turned his gaze onto Will. Kyle. Hell, he didn't even know what to call him.

Kyle was slumped in the chair, his handcuffed

hands behind him, his expression devoid of emotion. His eyes looked flat, his mouth a straight line, his posture radiating that he didn't give a damn what evidence they had against him.

Then he noticed a slight jiggle to the teenager's foot.

His heart began to race. Will used to jiggle his leg like that when he was nervous. At the spelling bee in school, at the rodeo when one of his favorite riders was about to perform, when he'd been in trouble at home.

He reminded himself that it was probably a common nervous gesture, but still hope took root in his chest.

Agent Cord dropped a file onto the table, then paced to the corner and stood, his arms crossed, his expression scrutinizing. Julie pulled out a chair and seated herself, a softness about her that made his body harden with desire.

"Kyle, that is your name, isn't it?" Julie said softly. "Or is it Will?"

Kyle shot her a go-to-hell look.

"The man that was with me, Brody Bloodworth, he thinks that you're his little brother. You see, his brother went missing seven years ago and Mr. Bloodworth hasn't seen him since."

Kyle simply stared at her, his expression cold again. "Yeah, so he said."

"It's true. Brody has hired private investigators and hounded the police and the FBI to keep looking for Will ever since he disappeared. But so far, that is until today, we have found zilch." Julie leaned back in the chair, relaxed, a small smile on her mouth. She was trying to win the boy's trust, make him feel safe, Brody realized.

Would it work?

"You see, Brody loved his brother a lot. Only he was a teenager and had a girlfriend, and one day they were at the rodeo and this girl convinced him to sneak out to an empty stall to make out." Julie's voice cracked a notch. "They left Will in the stands watching the rodeo, but when they got back he was gone."

Kyle's leg jiggled again. "Why you telling me all this, lady?"

Brody took a deep breath.

"Because I was that teenage girl with Brody," she said. "I'm Julie, I was Brody's friend back then. And I knew Will. I played horseshoes with Will at his ranch. And I helped him with math homework. Will also tagged along with me and Brody when we went fishing and took the boat out on the lake. Do you remember any of that?"

"How can I remember something that never happened?" Kyle said, his lips pressed in a thin line.

"Maybe you don't remember," Julie said, emotions tingeing her voice. "But Brody and I do. We both felt horrible about what happened that day at the rodeo. We went crazy searching for Will. Brody and his friends organized search parties day and night looking for him." She paused. "And Will's father went on TV pleading for people to come forward if they had any information. He wasn't rich by any means, but he posted a reward for information leading to Will's abduction."

Kyle dropped his gaze to the floor, but his jaw twitched.

"People offered leads, but none of them panned out," Julie continued. "Still, your brother never gave up."

He squeezed his eyes together, then righted his head, but didn't speak.

Julie reached out and touched his shoulder gently. "I want you to know that if you are Will, that we've both been looking for you. That if you are Will, you can tell us." She hesitated, then touched the file. "And if you're not, well, you remind us of him, and we want to help you anyway."

A small flicker of some emotion Brody couldn't define darkened Kyle's eyes for a brief second before that steely mask slid back down.

Agent Cord gave Julie an odd look as if he was surprised to hear that Julie had known Brody, then he walked over and slapped the table. "Look, kid, she might have a bleeding heart," he said, gesturing toward Julie. "But I don't. You know we caught you red-handed in an armed robbery. That's a felony itself, but tack on the hostage situation and you're looking at a lot of prison time."

Kyle shifted and stretched his legs out in front of him.

"You can do yourself a favor by cooperating," Agent Cord said.

"It does look bad," Julie said. "But there are always extenuating circumstances. Say, if someone forced you to commit that crime."

Brody sucked in a breath, hoping that Will would speak up, but he simply stared at the floor.

Agent Cord opened the file and spread several photos of the robberies across the table. "We have footage from three different convenience stores proving you were present at the robberies."

Kyle glanced at the pictures, his face stoic.

"Kyle," Julie said. "I know you didn't plan this robbery alone. Are you involved in a gang?"

That question brought a sharp look toward Julie.

"No gang?" she asked. "But each time you're with another boy close to your age. This boy here—" She pointed to the blond kid. "We believe his name is Tray Goodner and that he was abducted five years ago from a carnival."

"The two of you committed these robberies together," Agent Cord said. "Who is your ringleader, Kyle?" Agent Cord hit the table again. "Or are you the leader?"

Kyle shot him a belligerent look.

"We know you're in trouble," Agent Cord said. "And that you need our help."

Julie reached out to touch his shoulder, but he jerked away.

"We want to help you," Julie said. "Did someone hurt you? Force you to rob the stores?"

He glared at her again.

"You have bruises on you, Kyle. How did you get those?"

"None of your damn business," Kyle muttered.

Julie and the other agent exchanged a look. "All right, I think it's time to call your parents," Julie said. "Give us their name and number."

Kyle's body went rigid.

"I'm sure they're probably worried about you," Julie continued. "They'll want to know you're safe."

"There's nobody to call." The boy ducked his head down, his lips set tight, an angry look marring his face.

"Please," Julie said. "If someone forced you and Tray to rob that store, then we can make a deal for you. And we can help reunite you with your real families."

"I don't know what you're talking about," Kyle said.

"Fine, don't talk." Agent Cord's voice was harsh.

"You're old enough to be tried as an adult. Is that what you want?"

The boy's leg jiggled again. Then Julie slid another photo from the file and laid it on the table. "Look at this, Kyle. This little boy's name is Hank Forte. He's only six years old."

Kyle's gaze cut to the picture, but he quickly glanced back down at the floor. In that split second, Brody detected pain and fear in his eyes.

"Hank's mother and father are devastated," Julie said. "They carried him to a local fair for the day. They were having fun, riding rides, playing games, eating cotton candy, but they turned their heads for a minute, and he disappeared." Julie pushed the photo toward him, forcing it into his line of vision. "Hank's parents can't sleep right now. They're terrified and worried, and I'm sure that Hank is terrified, too."

Kyle flinched, a movement so small it was barely detectable. But it indicated that Julie was getting to him.

"If you know where he is, please tell us," Julie said softly. "You may think it's too late for you, but it's not. And if you talk to us, you can not only save yourself, but you can save Hank."

JULIE STRUGGLED TO control her voice. She was determined to present a calm front to Kyle. God only knew what the poor boy had gone through.

It was obvious that he'd been abused. Probably over a long period of time.

He was also lying. That she had no doubt about. Although he tried to look tough he was scared.

And not just for himself.

The tiny flinch at the corner of his mouth when she'd shown him that photo of Hank indicated he had seen the boy. That she was right about their abductor being the same unsub.

And that he understood the boy's terror.

So why wouldn't he help them?

He'd said he didn't have family, suggesting he lived on the streets.

That would be motivation for him to steal. He and Tray could have escaped together.

But she didn't think that was the case. Kyle seemed terrified when she'd mentioned calling his parents, meaning there must be someone where he lived that lorded over him.

Someone who wouldn't be happy the TBI had him in custody. And thanks to the damn press, he probably knew.

Kyle shifted and continued to stare at his feet, the bruises on his face more stark under the fluorescent light.

Agent Cord's phone buzzed, and he snatched up the file. "Think about that little boy Hank and how frightened he is, and how much his folks miss him and want him back while you spend the night in a cell."

The boy cut his eyes toward her, his silence thick with fear.

Julie stood, anxious to comfort him, but she couldn't. He was under arrest and had held a girl at gunpoint. Besides, judging from his body language, he wouldn't welcome being coddled.

A beating he would probably understand.

But she didn't intend to let that happen to him again.

"Please, Kyle. I really do want to help you," she said. "I also want to save Tray and Hank and however many boys this person stole from their homes. But you have to open up to me, trust me."

His handcuffs rattled as he twisted in his seat. "Just put me in my cell."

Julie stared at him for a long minute, willing him to change his mind. But he remained motionless, determined to keep his silence.

Finally she swallowed back her frustration, then nodded and headed to the door. But she paused and glanced at him one more time before she left the room. "The offer stands, Kyle. Whenever you're ready to talk, just tell the guard you want to see me, and I'll come as soon as I can."

He didn't respond, and she left the room, her stomach rolling as she went to see Brody.

When she entered the room, worry and pain etched his face. "What do you think?"

Julie wanted to lie and tell him everything would be all right, but they'd been through too much the past few years for her to do that. So she told him the truth.

"I think he's lying, that he knows where Hank is. That he and Tray were both abducted by the same man."

Brody cursed. "Then why won't he tell us who kidnapped him and the others?"

Julie didn't like the answers that crept into her mind. "Either he's suffering from Stockholm syndrome. It's when a kidnapped victim—"

"I know what is it," Brody said, cutting her off.

Julie nodded. "Or he's afraid that if he talks, his abductor will hurt the other boys he's still holding hostage."

Chapter Seven

"What do we do now?" Brody asked.

Julie sighed. "Unfortunately we'll have to leave him locked up for tonight. Maybe spending the night in a cell will convince him to talk."

Brody shook his head. "I doubt it. A night in a cell may be a reprieve from what he's endured these past few years."

Julie winced. "I hate to say it, but you may be right."

Brody scrubbed a hand over his face. "I can't stand to see him like that, handcuffed and in a cell, not after all he's suffered. I always thought when I found him, he'd be glad to see me and I'd bring him home."

Julie rubbed his arm in a comforting gesture. "I know it's difficult, but at least he's alive, Brody. That means you have a chance to bring him home someday."

Brody turned to her, praying that he could do just that. "What happens if he doesn't talk?"

"I'm going to insist on both a physical exam and a psych evaluation," Julie said. "Hopefully we can use that in court to avoid going to trial until we know all the details about Kyle's abductor and catch this maniac."

Brody latched onto that hope. If he could just take the teenager to the BBL, maybe he could breach that armor Will had erected to protect himself.

"Let me make some calls."

She started to step out of the room, and Brody caught her arm. "Thanks, Julie. I…appreciate everything you're doing."

Her beautiful eyes glittered with emotions. "You don't have to thank me, Brody. I want Will home with you where he belongs, and I want the man who took him to rot in prison for the rest of his life."

Brody nodded, the years falling away as a hint of the old Julie returned. But the pain and guilt in her voice reminded him of the chasm between them. That losing Will had torn them apart.

Would finding him bring them back together again?

Julie stepped from the room, and he glanced through the window at the troubled, angry boy in the interrogation room, and thoughts of a reunion with Julie fled.

All that mattered was reaching his brother and

finding out who'd kidnapped him and turned him into a criminal.

Then he'd make the bastard pay.

After that, he had to help Will heal from the trauma he'd suffered over the years.

Of course, Will—Kyle—hadn't acknowledged that he recognized him, but deep in his gut, Brody knew this boy was his little brother. What had his abductor told him about his family?

Brody had told Will that he'd looked for him for years, but the boy had shown no reaction.

But somewhere deep down he had to know that Brody had never given up the search and that he loved him.

And if he didn't, Brody would make sure that he told him every day for the rest of his life until he believed him.

JULIE CORNERED AGENT Cord in the break room. "We have to get a medical and psych exam. That boy has been severely abused."

"I agree," Agent Cord said. "But I'm not so sure he's not the leader of a gang."

Julie clenched her teeth. "It's possible, but he's scared, which indicates he has someone to report to, someone he's afraid of."

"You think he recognized Hank Forte?"

Julie nodded. "He put on a face of steel, but he definitely reacted to the boy's picture."

Brody curled his hands into fists. "Then he should tell us where the unsub is keeping him."

Julie sighed and ran her hand through her hair. "Maybe he's afraid the creep will hurt Hank if he tells."

"So how do you suggest we approach the situation?" Agent Cord asked.

"Let's get the medical evaluations and maybe the judge will release him to a mental health facility. Counselors might be able to convince him to open up. But we have to remember, he's undergone seven years of intense abuse. It may take time for them to earn his trust enough for that to happen."

Agent Cord agreed and Julie stepped aside to call and make the arrangements. Brody's suffering drove her to take one last stab at Kyle, so she went back into the room. He was still sitting in the same chair, arms behind his back, his expression closed. Bleak.

His bruises had darkened to an ugly purple. Those were the ones she could see. He had so many others inside, ones maybe even deeper and more painful than the visible ones on his body.

Her heart ached for him. Had he had any kind of affection the past few years?

Probably not, she thought sadly. His only physical contact had most likely been at the other end of the kidnapper's fist.

"I want to explain what's going to happen," Julie said matter-of-factly. "You'll spend the night in the cell," she said. "In the morning, you're going to be given a physical exam by a doctor, then a psychiatrist is going to speak with you."

A belligerent look twisted his face.

"Remember, I'm on your side," Julie said. "I'll do whatever I can for you. And if you help us find the person who kidnapped you, who took little Hank Forte from his mama and daddy, then we can make these charges against you disappear."

For a hairbreadth of a second, he looked at her as if he wanted to talk. Then that hardened look passed over him again, and he stared at the floor.

Julie sighed then reached for the doorknob. "All you have to do is ask for me and I'll come to your assistance. Any time of day or night."

She waited another second, hoping, praying he'd talk to her, but he didn't respond, so she left the room, her heart heavy.

If this boy had been severely abused as she strongly suspected, the last thing he needed was to be locked up, to be caged like a wild animal. But her hands were tied.

And like she'd told Brody, earning his trust would take time.

And poor little Hank…What was happening to him right now?

BRODY FROWNED as Agent Cord ordered Will—he had to call him Kyle for now—to stand up. "Let's go."

Kyle kept his head down, but his body was tense, and a muscle ticked in his jaw. Kyle was upset, scared. Maybe worried about the other boy who'd been with him.

They exited the room, and Brody did the same. He was only a few feet from his brother. Dammit, he wanted to haul him up for a bear hug and assure him everything would be all right.

But when he took a step toward him, Kyle stiffened and gave him a look of pure hatred. Then suddenly the elevator opened and a man and woman rushed into the hallway, looking harried and frantic.

Hank Forte's parents—Brody recognized them from the newscast.

"Is this the boy?" the woman shrieked as she and her husband raced toward Kyle.

"It is, you're the one who robbed that store," the man shouted.

Kyle jerked his head up, for the first time since he'd been arrested, real emotions flitting across his face. Panic. And...something else. Pain.

Mrs. Forte grabbed at him. "The officer in Amarillo said you might know where our little boy is."

"Please, son, tell us," Mr. Forte said.

Julie suddenly rushed toward them. "Mr. and Mrs. Forte, please—"

"Please what?" Mrs. Forte whirled around at Julie. "Don't ask him about our child?"

Agent Cord cleared his throat and placed an arm between Kyle and the couple to keep them from grabbing him. "Let us handle this."

Mrs. Forte slapped at Julie's hands, tears streaming down her face. "But if he knows, why won't he tell us? Why would he protect a monster who'd steal a child from his parents?"

"Do you know where he is?" Mr. Forte asked harshly.

Kyle's jaw tightened in reaction, but he jerked his head to the side to avoid looking at them.

Julie cut her eyes toward the other agent. "Take him to his cell now. I'll handle this."

Both the Fortes lunged toward Kyle. "Tell us, have you seen our boy? Is he alive?" Mrs. Forte cried.

"Is he hurt?" Mr. Forte asked in a broken voice. "Who took him? What is he doing to him?"

"Please," Mrs. Forte pleaded as she burst into sobs. "Please, we miss him so much, he's just a little fellow, so innocent, we want to see him grow up…"

Brody's lungs squeezed for air. The questions, the pain and grief, the fear in the parents' voices, that desperation…he'd felt it for years.

"Will, please," Brody said, causing the boy to flinch again. "Tell us who took you. And if he has this little boy Hank, for God's sakes, speak up. These people want their son back just like I wanted you back."

Another tormented look crossed Kyle's face, his shoulders so rigid that Brody sensed his turmoil.

But then he sucked back any emotion and shuffled forward. "Take me to my cell."

Agent Cord took his elbow and herded him down the hall. Mrs. Forte began to sob, and her husband started to chase after Kyle and the agent.

"Stop, please tell us where he is. Don't protect that monster!"

Brody had stood in the background long enough. Mrs. Forte started to run after her husband, but Julie caught her. "Mrs. Forte, let's go sit down and talk."

Brody caught up with the man and stepped in front of him to keep him from attacking Kyle. "Mr. Forte, we need to talk. Come on back here with your wife."

"Do you know where my son is?" Mr. Forte screeched. "Because if you don't, let me talk to that kid."

Brody ached for the man, but he also hurt for Kyle. Something was keeping him from telling the truth. Fear. Trauma. Maybe he'd been brainwashed....

Kyle and the agent disappeared through a set

of double doors, and Mr. Forte bent over, heaving for a breath.

Brody patted his back. "I understand what you're going through, I really do."

"How could you know?" he said angrily.

Brody swallowed hard, then gripped the man's elbow and guided him back toward Julie and Mrs. Forte. "Because my little brother was kidnapped seven years ago," Brody said.

The man turned tear-stained eyes up toward him. "He was?"

"Yes." Brody stopped in front of Julie, and Mrs. Forte reached for her husband, obviously needing his support.

Then she looked up at Brody with wide, imploring eyes. "Your brother," she said, her voice cracking, "did you ever find him?"

Brody and Julie exchanged concerned looks, then Julie gestured for them to go into the break room with them. "Sit down, and I'll get you some water," she said gently.

Mrs. Forte stumbled into a chair and her husband sank down beside her. "Did you find him?" Mrs. Forte asked again.

Julie rushed to get them some water while Brody sat down and began to explain.

THIRTY MINUTES LATER, the Fortes had calmed from anger to shock to resignation. But the fear lingered, cold and so real that it tainted the air with the realization that a little boy had been ripped from his home and wouldn't be sleeping safely in his own bed that night.

Julie had to offer them hope.

"If Kyle was abducted by the same person who took your son, then the fact that he is still alive is a good sign." She patted the woman's shoulder.

"You mean that Hank is still alive?" Mr. Forte asked, wiping at his eyes.

"Yes." Julie knew it wasn't much, just a crumb, but they needed any positive encouragement they could get.

She glanced at Brody and offered him a sympathetic smile. He'd poured out his heart to soothe the couple yet he was also hurting.

Mrs. Forte turned to Brody with a pleading look. "You think that teenager is your brother?"

Brody hesitated, then gave a clipped nod. "I don't know what he's been through, but I'm going to find out."

"Why won't he talk to you?" Mr. Forte asked. "If some monster kidnapped him and hurt him, it seems like he'd want to turn him in. That he'd want to help our Hank from suffering like that."

Pain slashed across Brody's chiseled face, and she decided not to point out the hard facts she'd learned in the bureau. That sometimes abused kids turned out to be abusers themselves.

Instead, Julie explained about Stockholm syndrome, then focused on another theory. "It's also possible that Kyle is not talking because he actually thinks he's protecting the other boys. And maybe he is. Maybe his abductor threatened to hurt Hank if he didn't come back with money for the family. And he most assuredly threatened to hurt him or any other children he's holding if Kyle talked."

"Oh, my God." Mr. Forte's eyes widened in horror. "How many do you think this monster has kidnapped?"

"We don't know yet," Julie said, an image of the other ten boys on the bulletin board in the conference room taunting her. "But I promise you that we will do everything we can to bring your son back home to you."

The couple clung to each other, nodding, accepting the hope she offered because they had nothing else to do. Because they wouldn't give up, just like Brody hadn't. Julie thought about other cases she'd worked, about her and Brody and the night Will had gone missing.

A large percentage of couples who lost children fell apart.

Just as she and Brody had.

She hoped this couple made it. If they found Hank, and she was determined that they would, he was going to need both of them to recover from his ordeal.

Just like Will needed Brody now. All the more reason Brody had to remain strong.

And all the more reason she had to remain focused on the case.

"You'll call us the minute he talks, the minute you know anything about our son?" Mr. Forte asked.

"Of course," Julie said. "I promise you I won't give up until I find him."

The couple stood, both trembling and holding on to one another, and she and Brody walked them to the elevator.

As soon as the doors closed behind them, Brody sighed, a pained sound that tore at her heart.

She looked over at him and wanted to take him in her arms and hold him, promise him everything would be all right.

But they'd both learned long ago that wishes didn't always come true, that bad things happened.

The fact that Will had disappeared proved it. The bruises on him and his cold, closed demeanor only reinforced that he'd suffered a severe trauma.

"I need to see him again before I go," Brody said.

"I'm not sure that's a good idea."

"Please, Julie. He's my kid brother and he's

been through hell. I just want to make sure he's all right."

Normally Julie would refuse, but this was Brody and she felt his pain as if it was her own. So she led him down the hall through another hall and an elevator that led to the holding cells.

Julie explained that Kyle would be confined until they finished interrogating him and then he'd be moved to a regular prison. Still, Brody tensed as she escorted him through security and they reached the cell.

She tried to see the place through Brody's eyes. To her, the TBI was business.

But she'd never had anyone she cared about locked inside, and she knew that could be unnerving.

Then she spotted Will in the cell and her stomach clenched. He was lying on the cot facing the wall, his body tucked almost in a fetal position.

"Will?" Brody said quietly.

But Will showed no response.

"I'm here if you want to talk."

Brody lingered, his tormented expression tearing at Julie.

"We're both here if you need us," Julie said.

"She's right," Brody said. "I won't let you down this time."

But Will still remained motionless, his face turned away from them.

Finally Brody released a deep sigh and Julie walked him back toward the elevator. He paused at the door, then wiped perspiration from his brow.

"God," Brody murmured in a choked whisper. "What did that bastard do to him?"

KYLE STARED at the scratches on the wall, counting them just like he did when he was at home. He had to do something to make his mind stop thinking.

His pulse began to pound, that sick feeling rising in his throat again. What would the people do to him here if he didn't talk?

But how could he?

If he told them about their father, the police would storm their compound. It was a compound, he'd decided a long time ago, not a home. The outbuildings where his father kept them were stalls like on a ranch. The floors dirt. The walls battered wood. Then concrete in their new compound. They hadn't been there long.

He was stupid to get caught. So stupid. Father would not tolerate his failure again. He'd punish him before he put him in the ground like he did the others who defied him.

His stomach clenched. He didn't care if he died. Sometimes he'd even begged for it.

Especially when he had to go in the hole.

He hated the dark pit. He couldn't breathe there, couldn't see or hear anything, couldn't do anything but think about the fear and fight the darkness…

He hadn't been there in a while. But the new brother was there now.

Suddenly he felt like he was suffocating again. He opened his mouth and struggled for a breath.

The hole was where you went when you were bad.

And he'd been bad a lot.

But he didn't want the others to suffer because he was bad now.

The pretty woman's face flashed in his mind. She had a soft voice. Eyes that reminded him of glittering stars. And a smile that reminded him of someone… Someone, but he didn't remember who.

She said his name was Will. That she'd known him long ago.

But his name wasn't Will. It was Kyle.

And that other man with the big cowboy hat. Brody Bloodworth.

He claimed he was his brother.

But that was wrong. His brothers lived on the compound. His father picked them because they were special. Because their families didn't want them anymore.

At least that's what he told the new ones.

Had he told him that when he'd first come to live with him? He didn't remember. All he remembered was the voice coming through the pipe in the hole…the voice telling him he was bad.

He closed his eyes, tried to think of a way to escape. He had to go home, beg his father not to hurt the little ones.

The cries of that woman, Hank's mama, and his daddy's questions reverberated in his head, and his eyes stung. They said their son had gone missing. That they loved him and wanted him back.

It was Hank.

He was the kid in the picture the lady had shown him.

The blond kid with the crooked teeth.

But Father said his name was Davis.

Still, the little boy had screamed that it was Hank. Over and over he'd cried that name.

Kyle curled his body tighter, wrapped his arms around his knees. He couldn't trust the police or these people. He couldn't trust anyone.

If his father even thought they were coming to the compound, he'd put them all in the hole. He might even leave them there and start his family over.

Just like he'd done before.

No, he couldn't tell the police or anyone.

He had to find a way to escape.

It was the only way he could save Hank and the others.

Chapter Eight

Brody couldn't sleep that night.

He and Julie had picked up burgers and carried them to their hotel, and he'd said good night to her at her room, then retreated to his own.

Alone.

Being near her again was playing havoc on his senses. Her sweet feminine smell, the way the light glowed off her golden hair making it look like silk, the husky sound of her voice when she spoke his name—all those things taunted him with what-ifs.

What if they had stuck together seven years ago? Would they have a family of their own now?

Would she be a TBI agent?

God, seeing her with that gun was sexy as hell. But it also instilled a fear in him that he didn't know how to deal with. Every time she went out on a case she put her life on the line.

Dammit. He poured a cup of coffee from the

pot in the room, then stared at the sunlight streaming through.

His thoughts turned to Will, and how desolate he'd looked lying on that cot. What was going on in his brother's mind? What had the person who'd kidnapped him done to him over the years?

Did Will's abductor have that little boy Hank?

Stories of sexual and physical abuse, compounded by psychological abuse, were rampant on the news. The scenarios that flashed in Brody's head made him vault from the bed and pace the room. Sweat beaded on his neck and bile rose to his throat.

Did Will remember him? Or was he too traumatized to ever find his way back and have a normal life?

And what if the court didn't show leniency and he went to jail? Armed robbery, and taking a hostage…he could spend years behind bars.

His life destroyed because some maniac had kidnapped him from the safety of his family at that damn rodeo.

Furious, he wanted to pound something.

Too agitated to rest, he jumped in the shower. On the way to the hotel the night before Julie had said that she'd asked for a court hearing this morning.

He had to be there. So did the lawyer he'd called when he'd closed himself in the hotel room. Ethan

Houser had come recommended to him by way of Carter Flagstone, one of his buddies who helped out at the BBL. He'd explained the circumstances and Ethan had jumped at the chance to handle the case and help him.

He quickly rinsed and dried off, then dressed and phoned his accountant. He wanted to make sure he had the funds available so he could post bail.

Maybe if they explained the situation to the judge, he would release Will into his custody and let Brody take him to the BBL.

JULIE GRABBED HER phone to call Brody, her body aching with fatigue. All night she'd wrestled with the demons in her head.

The children who'd been stolen from their families—first Will, then the other cases she'd worked, then the boys they suspected had been kidnapped by the same person who'd abducted Will.

The world had so much evil in it. One case after another, one monster after another. Would it ever end?

Shaking off the desolation, she channeled her emotions to the back burner just as she'd done for years. She wanted a meeting to discuss strategy before she met with the judge. She punched Brody's number, tapping her foot while she waited.

He must have been sitting on the phone because he answered on the first ring.

"I'm heading to the TBI headquarters. Are you ready to go?"

"Yes. I'll be there in a second."

Julie brushed through her hair, pulling it back in a loose bun at the nape of her neck then straightened her jacket. Thankfully she kept an overnight bag in her car with a change of clothes since she never knew how long she'd be gone when she left her apartment.

A knock sounded at the door, and she opened it to find Brody freshly shaven but wearing the same clothes.

"Ready?"

She nodded, grabbed her purse and they headed to her car.

"If we have to be here any longer, I'll need to get some more clothes," Brody said.

Julie climbed in the car and started the engine. "We'll see." She didn't want to make promises she couldn't keep. She'd already disappointed Brody too much in their lifetime.

"What's going to happen today?" Brody finally asked.

"Kyle is going to be evaluated by a physician and a psychiatrist this morning. I'll meet with the task force about this case and the other kidnappings. After lunch, we'll meet with the judge for Kyle's arraignment."

"I called my accountant to arrange to have money available to post bail," Brody said.

Julie glanced at him but refrained from comment. She'd read that he'd done well for himself, that he was wealthy. And she knew it was true just by looking at the BBL.

He didn't look wealthy though—he looked like a stronger, tougher image of the boy she had once loved with all her heart. A cowboy through and through. A man with a code of honor she'd always admired.

They lapsed into silence again, covering the short distance to the headquarters in no time. When they got inside, Agent Cord informed them that Kyle was meeting with the psychiatrist.

"I think we should review all the cases involving these missing boys," Julie said. She'd stayed up researching them half the night.

Agent Cord frowned as they headed into the conference room, and gestured toward Brody. "Do you think he should be here? This is official business."

Julie tensed, well aware that Brody heard Cord's comment. "Yes. If Kyle is really Will, it might help Brody to know about some of the other boys abducted. If he could convince him to talk about them, even one of them, it would confirm that the cases are really connected."

Agent Cord nodded in concession. "I suppose that's true."

They filed into the room where Chief Hurt was already waiting. At Brody's request, his friend Miles McGregor had been called in to work the task force, as well.

Brody walked over to him and the men shook hands. "Thanks for being here, Miles."

"No problem." Miles glanced at the photos of the kids on the wall. "This unsub has to be stopped."

Chief Hurt cleared his throat then asked everyone to sit down.

Then Julie took the lead. "I've been studying all of these cases and want us to review them again." She gestured toward Chief Hurt. "Did you find out anything from interviewing the staff at the locations we discussed?"

"What locations?" Brody asked.

Julie pointed to the board with the map and pushpins. "We've tagged each spot where the boys disappeared. Mostly public places, a rodeo, park, carnival and county fair. At least those are the most recent."

"We're still working that angle," Chief Hurt said. "So far, we haven't found a commonality between the employees. But we'll keep digging."

Julie walked over to a whiteboard and drew a line. "I've been thinking about our unsub and these cases. If they are connected, the crimes were committed by one kidnapper, which means he started when he was young. Often serial offenders are in their twenties." She made a note of it on the board in one corner. "That means he would be in his forties now." She paused again. "We don't know his trigger for the first abduction. The most plausible reason would be that he lost a child and needed to fill that void."

"Or he could be a pedophile who simply likes kids," Agent Cord cut in.

Julie sighed. "That's possible. The doctor examining Kyle may be able to tell us more."

A muscle ticked in Brody's jaw, but she resisted sugarcoating the truth. They had to face reality.

Beside, if Kyle, Will, had been sexually abused, they needed to know so a psychiatrist or counselor could treat him properly.

"The fact that Kyle is still alive is a positive sign," Julie said. "It means our unsub keeps his victims alive. But it also raises questions." She pointed to the photographs. "We have a total of ten unsolved cases that fit the profile. How can the unsub hide ten kids? Are they in school? If he's abusing them, how has he kept neighbors from seeing them?"

"He has to live somewhere off the grid," Chief Cord said. "Maybe a farm with a lot of acres."

Julie nodded. "But feeding that many boys, especially teenagers, is expensive, especially if he has a menial job, which, if he worked at the locations where he abducted his victims, is likely."

"Let's review the list of victims and see if anything clicks. First, Jeremy Unger went missing from a park twenty years ago. He was seven then so now he would be twenty-seven."

"How do you force a twenty-seven-year-old to stay and not fight back?" Brody asked.

Julie frowned. "Stockholm syndrome, abuse, fear," Julie said. "Next, Carl Fanning disappeared eighteen years ago from a birthday party at a public pool. He was five, meaning he would be twenty-three now." She scribbled the information on the time line, then continued.

"Fifteen years ago, Daryl Derwin went missing from a ball park. He was six, meaning he would be twenty-one now."

Agent Hurt shifted. "From what we know about this type of predator, he likes victims around a certain age. Other cases show that it's usually preadolescent boys. If he's keeping them longer, it may not be sexual."

"Or he may be killing them when they reach a certain age," Agent Cord said.

"But Kyle is seventeen, and he's still alive," Miles interjected.

"And the kid with Kyle in the robberies looks to be around thirteen or fourteen."

Julie scratched her head in thought, then jotted the theories in the corner of the board. Something wasn't fitting.

"Okay, let's go on," she said as she drew another line. "Anthony Putnam disappeared ten years ago from a local festival when he was five, meaning he would be fifteen now." She moved to the next one. "Jeff Wickman went missing from a bingo game at a rec center when he was seven. That was six years ago, meaning he would be thirteen." She took a breath. "Six years ago, Phil Jasper disappeared from a horse show. He was six, so he would be twelve.

"Seven years ago, Will Bloodworth disappeared from a rodeo. He was ten, now seventeen." She tacked the next photo on the time line.

"Five years ago, Tray Goodner, the boy who committed the robberies with Kyle, was taken from a carnival in San Antonio. He was eight, so he's thirteen now."

"Two years ago, Lewis Renz was abducted from a camp. He was eight, making him ten now. Then Hank Forte disappeared at a county fair. He's six and as far as we know, the latest victim."

"There are some lags in the time line," Chief Hurt pointed out.

Julie nodded. "It could mean someone got close to finding him, and he had to lay low. Or he was satisfied for a while then needed a new conquest."

A knock sounded on the door, then one of the forensic techs poked her head in. "I have the results from the medical examination and the psych one, as well."

"What about the DNA results for Kyle?"

"They're in there, too."

Julie tensed, her gaze meeting Brody's. She needed this information to plan her approach to the judge.

And she wanted this boy to be Will Bloodworth so Brody would have him back.

Although even if it was Will, he might never be the same boy Brody had known as a child.

BRODY TOOK A deep breath. He wanted his brother back.

But he wasn't sure he really wanted to know what he'd suffered.

You have to, he reminded himself sternly. *You can't help him unless you know everything.*

"Brody?" Julie asked.

"Go ahead and read it," he said gruffly.

Julie opened the file and skimmed over it, then looked at Brody. "First the DNA."

Several strained heartbeats passed, the air vibrating with tension. Brody gripped the edges of his chair, desperate to know the truth.

Finally Julie lifted her head and looked at him, "Kyle is Will Bloodworth." She offered Brody a smile, but the air around him suddenly felt hot. "He's your brother, Brody. We finally found him."

Brody's throat thickened with emotions, and he couldn't help himself. He crossed the room and pulled Julie into a hug. She wrapped her arms around him, and he felt her tears dampen his shirt.

Joy blended with the fear and sorrow in his chest. He had waited for this moment for so long. Had almost given up so many times.

Had imagined Will dead.

But now he was here, alive.

He blinked back his own tears, and Julie sniffled, then slowly pulled away. Embarrassment at his display shot through him, but then decided he didn't give a damn.

An uncomfortable silence reverberated through the room, the whisper of clothing rustling as everyone shifted.

Miles rose and pounded him on the back. "You said you'd find him and you did, Brody."

Brody nodded, too moved to speak.

Chief Hurt made a noise in his throat, and Brody and Miles both claimed their seats again.

"All right, now we know one more thing about

our unsub," Chief Hurt said. "He gives the boys new names."

Agent Cord drummed his fingers on the conference table. "What else does the report say, Julie?"

She wiped at her eyes, then composed herself, although her hand trembled as she scanned the file again. A frown puckered between her brows and Brody held his breath, bracing himself for bad news.

THE POLICE had Kyle in custody. They would hammer him with questions, try to find out about him and where his family lived.

He had taught the boy to guard his family, that protecting them at all costs was his job. Kyle was one of his best soldiers. He was tough, skills honed, could endure pain or whatever the enemy threw at him.

The boy knew the law was the enemy. If the police discovered where the family lived, they would tear them apart, their army of men.

Kyle had been stupid to get caught.

Still, he wouldn't talk.

The newest member of his squadron yelled and beat at the door to the pit.

He was weak now, but his training would change that.

Maybe it was time to move again.

He would start looking for a new place to house his team today.

And if Kyle utilized the skills he'd taught him, he would find a way to come back to them again.

If not, he'd make sure he didn't talk.

Not ever again.

Chapter Nine

Brody's stomach knotted as Julie read the doctors evaluation. "The psychiatrist said Kyle—Will—was uncommunicative, that he refused to talk about where he lived, about any abductions or the other boys, or anything that had happened to him. He exhibited signs of physical and mental abuse, and signs of sensory deprivation, as well, and seemed especially sensitive to darkness and oddly, also to bright lights. She also observed that he assumed a military stance when she entered the room and when the guard appeared to take him from his cell."

"So the unsub may have had military training," Agent Cord said. "That could help."

Julie nodded, then licked her lips, her expression odd. Brody's chest was beating so hard he could barely breathe.

"The doctor confirms that there has been long-term physical abuse," Julie said. "There are signs of bruises, repeated beatings, and broken bones but there was no sign of sexual abuse or molestation."

A mixture of anguish, anger and relief filled Brody. The thought of physical abuse sickened him, but at least Will hadn't been molested. Still he'd suffered...how had his little brother survived?

"If the unsub doesn't sexually abuse them, then what is his deal?" Agent Hurt asked. "Why is he fixated on kidnapping young boys?"

Brody scrubbed a hand over his face. The only one who could answer that was his brother. And Will wasn't talking.

"Good question," Julie said. She turned to the time line again. "The first kidnapping was probably personal. Perhaps the unsub had a child and lost it to death or his wife ran off with the child and left. He wanted a replacement."

"But what about the military angle?" Agent Cord asked.

Julie chewed her bottom lip in thought. "We can theorize all day and not get it right. But think about it. What if he lost the child while he was in the service? Maybe his wife left him while he was deployed?"

"You could look at it another way," Brody said. "If he was in combat, maybe he saw some fellow young men die."

"Or he was responsible for a child's death," Miles interjected.

"He could be suffering from PTSD," Chief Hurt pointed out.

"Or it's a combination," Julie said. "He was deployed and his child either died or his wife ran off with the child while he was overseas. He comes home expecting to have his family waiting. He's suffered, maybe injured, has PTSD and his family is suddenly gone. He looks for them but can't find them and has to replace his son." She paused. "So he takes victim number one, Jeremy Unger."

A quiet descended through the room, the tension palpable. Then Julie snapped her fingers. "Since we think that the first abduction was personal, and we know that he gives the boys new names when he captures them, let's look closer at Jeremy.

"He was seven when he was abducted, which tells us that the unsub's son, or the child that was lost, was around that age. Let's investigate that theory." She turned to Agent Cord. "Why don't you run a check on any children between six and eight who died around that time? Go back six months, a year."

"Since this was the first victim, the unsub probably lived near the site where the kidnapping took place," Chief Hurt suggested.

"That was twenty years ago," Agent Cord cut in. "The police probably already questioned everyone who lived near there."

"But they were looking for witnesses," Julie said. "Review the old case file. The technical analyst can help us search medical records for children who died within that time frame. Also, have her look at divorce records, specifically ones where a child was involved. You might even have her search the name Jeremy, or at least have her run his photo against photos of any children who died or were separated from their father."

Agent Cord reached for his iPad. "I'm on it. And I'll also ask the analyst to cross-reference with men who were released from military service around that time period."

Julie nodded. "Good thinking."

"I'll keep looking at the workers who might have held jobs in the areas near the attacks," Chief Hurt said.

Julie nodded. "And I'll work with Brody to see if we can get through to Will."

Brody gritted his teeth. Hopefully the agents knew what they were doing.

He only wished he did, that he knew how to reach his brother.

Julie checked her watch. "Come on, Brody, it's time to meet with the judge."

His chest clenched again. What if the judge refused to release Will and made him go to prison until his trial? Judging from what he'd been through, locking him up would only force him deeper into that silent shell. That was the only way he had coped, Brody realized with a pang to his chest.

So setting Will free was the only way he'd ever get close enough to him to convince him to talk.

The lawyer he'd hired to defend Will met him at the courthouse, and Brody pulled him aside and explained the doctors reports.

Ethan glanced at Julie. "What are you planning to do?"

Julie offered a tentative smile. "Request that he be released into my custody. We need his help, and he doesn't deserve to be locked up right now."

"I have bail money ready to go," Brody said.

Satisfied with their strategy, they filed into the courtroom for the arraignment and took their seats. Brody's heart stuttered as the guard opened the door and another guard escorted his brother inside the courtroom, handcuffed and shackled.

Brody searched Will's face, a bone-deep ache consuming him at how rigidly he walked, at the tough bravado on his face.

And the bruises on his body.

Will sank into the chair on the other side of Julie, a dead look in his eyes.

Brody scrubbed a hand across his face. If he found out who had put those bruises on his brother, he wouldn't ask questions.

He'd make the bastard feel the same kind of pain he'd inflicted on Will.

JULIE SPOTTED District Attorney Byron Stewart and inwardly winced. He was a thirty-five-year-old edgy man with a harsh attitude and an unforgiving spirit. She'd rarely seen him show pity on anyone.

It didn't bode well for Will today.

"We're going to try to convince the judge to release you into my custody," she said quietly to Will.

He didn't respond, simply sat stiffly as if expecting to be punished.

Her heart bled as she imagined all he'd endured. He'd probably been taught that fighting back only made the punishment worse.

Ten minutes later, she feared they were in real trouble.

D.A. Stewart presented photo after photo of Will and Tray Goodner robbing three different convenience stores.

"Your Honor, this young man is dangerous. He held a young woman hostage and, judging from this behavior, would have killed her if police hadn't intervened."

"Objection, conjecture," Ethan Houser said. "The district attorney cannot predict what my client would or would not have done."

Stewart rounded on Houser with a shocked look. "Your Honor—"

"The gun was not loaded," Houser added.

"The young woman and the police didn't know that," Stewart snapped.

Julie stood. "Your Honor, may I please speak?"

The judge adjusted his bifocals. "You have evidence to show me?"

Julie nodded. "May we approach the bench?"

His eyebrows furrowed, but he nodded and gestured for Stewart and Houser to join her.

"Your Honor, I find this highly objectionable," D.A. Stewart said, slanting Julie a cynical look. "Special Agent Whitehead has spearheaded this investigation and assisted in collecting evidence against the young man in custody. And now she's trying to get him off?"

"That is not my intention, Your Honor," Julie said. "But there are extenuating circumstances that you should be aware of."

He rubbed his forehead. "I'm listening."

Julie took a deep breath. "We have just learned that this young man, Kyle, is really Will Bloodworth, a boy who was kidnapped when he was ten years old." She explained about the doctors reports and the connection to the other kidnappings. "We believe that he is traumatized, but that he may be able to lead us to his abductor and to

Hank Forte, the six-year-old child who was kidnapped this week."

"Then leave him in jail and have a counselor work with him there," D.A. Stewart said.

"The young man has been severely abused and traumatized," Julie said. "Locking him up is cruel and unusual punishment."

"He committed armed robbery and held a girl at gunpoint," Stewart hissed.

"With an unloaded gun," Houser added.

"Judge," Julie continued. "There is much more at stake here than the robberies. We're talking about solving a serial kidnapping case that spans a twenty-year-old time frame, and finding out what happened to nine other missing children. In fact, it is our belief that Will Bloodworth's life has been threatened, and that the other children, if they are still alive, may be in extreme danger. The fact that the press showed Will's photograph on screen could trigger this unsub to try to run, and to get rid of any evidence of his crimes, including the children he stole. Time is of the essence."

"Judge," D.A. Stewart argued. "These dramatics are out of line. You can't release this young man. He's dangerous."

Julie pivoted toward the D.A. "What do you think is happening to the other children this man is holding hostage?"

The D.A. opened his mouth to object, but the

judge threw up his hand. "I've heard enough." He glanced down at the files, skimming over the reports Julie had provided.

When he looked back up, a deep frown marred his face.

"What do you propose we do?" the judge asked. "I can't release him on his own."

"His older brother, Brody Bloodworth, is here, Your Honor. He's been searching for his brother for years. He's not only a respectable member of society, but he owns a ranch called the Bucking Bronc Lodge. The BBL is designed to help young boys and men in trouble, and is equipped with on-site counseling services."

The judge's eyes flickered with recognition. "I've heard of the BBL." He glanced over at Brody with a quick smile.

"I will also be monitoring him," Julie added. "You can release him into my custody. Together with Mr. Bloodworth, I believe we can convince Will to lead us to his captor and to Hank Forte."

Julie held her breath while she waited on his response. A moment later, he gave a short nod then gestured for them to take their seats. The D.A. gave her a disapproving look as she went to stand beside Will. Brody looked anxious, but Will still sat rigid, his expression stony.

Julie said a silent prayer that the judge agreed

with her. If Will had to return to jail, she was afraid they would lose any chance of him talking.

BRODY'S LUNGS churned for air as he waited on the judge to answer. He'd tried to hear what Julie and the D.A. were saying, but they had spoken in hushed voices.

But Julie was fighting to save his brother.

His admiration for her mounted. He had loved her so much when they were young. And as much as he hated her job, he was impressed with her tough, professional demeanor. She was a powerful advocate when she cared about something.

The judge pounded his gavel and the bailiff gestured for them to rise to hear his decision. "After evaluating the evidence in this case and considering the extenuating circumstances," the judge said, "I have decided to release Kyle into the custody of Special Agent Julie Whitehead with the stipulation that he remain in her care and that he reside on the BBL with supervision by Mr. Bloodworth." He angled himself toward Will. "But know this, young man, if you attempt to escape from them or do not cooperate and undergo counseling as mandated by this court, you will be returned to jail until time for your trial. Do you understand?"

Will squared his shoulders, but a flicker of some emotion Brody didn't understand registered in his brother's eyes.

"I asked you a question, young man," the judge said in a firm voice. "Do you understand?"

Will's lips pinched tightly together. "Sir, yes, sir."

The judge studied him for a moment then looked at Brody. "Bail is set at a hundred thousand dollars. You can pay the clerk outside." He turned to Julie. "I hope you know what you're doing, Special Agent Whitehead."

"Yes, sir," Julie said.

He pounded the gavel, then dismissed them. Ethan shook Brody's hand. "I'll let you know when the trial date is set. And I'll need to speak to my client before then."

"We'll stay in touch," Brody said. "Just see that the trial date is postponed until we have a chance to get some answers."

"Of course." Ethan reached out to pat Will's shoulder, but Will stiffened and moved away from him.

Brody's heart ached. He would do everything he could for his brother.

He just hoped it would be enough.

The guard removed Will's handcuffs, but Will remained rigid as if he'd just been sentenced to another cell.

"Come on, Kyle," Julie said softly as she took his arm. "We're taking you to Brody's ranch."

Will frowned, and Brody wondered when would

be the best time to tell him about the DNA test. Ethan flanked Julie on one side while he walked beside Will, the four of them leaving the court-room at the same time.

Brody went to pay the clerk the bail money, then joined the trio again and they headed down the hall, then outside.

He gritted his teeth when two reporters shot for-ward, mikes extended, cameras flashing. "Special Agent Whitehead, we heard you arrested one of the boys in the gang of robberies?"

"Son, why did you do it?" the other reporter asked.

The first reporter shoved the mike at Julie. "Are you releasing him?"

Julie's expression tightened, and Will dropped his head in an attempt to avoid the camera. "Yes, we made an arrest but the investigation is ongo-ing, and I can't comment on it at this time."

Reporter one bristled. "Mr. Bloodworth, you run the BBL. What is your relationship to the de-fendant?"

Brody glanced at Will and saw his jaw flinch slightly. He couldn't divulge the truth to the public before Will knew. Neither did he want to reveal where he was taking Will in case his kidnapper came after him. "No comment."

Ethan stepped up. "Excuse us. We're done with this interview for now."

The reporters both opened their mouths to ask more questions, but Ethan quickly herded Julie, Will and him toward the car.

Will's posture remained rigid as they stepped outside, but his eyes scanned the streets as if he was looking for someone.

Or for a way to escape.

Brody grimaced. He'd have to watch him on the ranch. He had a feeling the first chance he got, Will would bolt and run away.

HE WATCHED THE NEWS interview with a scowl. Son of a bitch.

How the hell had Brody Bloodworth found Kyle?

He bunched his hands into fists. If he was taking him back with him to that ranch, it meant he knew who he was.

And he would drill Kyle until he remembered what happened that day at the rodeo.

If anyone could break Kyle, it was his brother.

Fury coiled inside him as he stood and went to the window. If Kyle broke and spilled his guts, he might lead them to the compound.

He couldn't let that happen. He'd moved before, but he liked it here. And every time he moved, he had to leave some of his family, his team behind.

Jeremy walked in the door and he explained what had happened.

"Don't worry, Father," Jeremy said. "I will take care of Kyle."

He smiled and patted Jeremy on the back. He had taught his son to obey and now he would.

Chapter Ten

The ride to the BBL was riddled with tension. Julie kept her eyes on the wheel and listened as Brody told Will about the BBL.

"It adjoins my property," Brody said. "It's definitely a working ranch so I have hired hands, but the boys who attend the camps also assist. The older boys, actually teens like yourself and some in their twenties, teach the younger ones how to ride, groom the horses and work with the cattle."

Will remained sullen as he stared out the window.

"We had a rodeo last year to raise money and had some big-name rodeo riders. One was a friend of mine—Johnny Long. The boys also made promotional signs for it and participated in riding, roping skills, barrel races and other events."

Other than a small frown that puckered between Will's dark eyebrows, he showed no reaction.

"I bet you're hungry." Julie glanced in the rearview mirror to see his response but he made none.

"I could eat a burger," Brody said.

"Me, too." Julie knew the area and found a steak-and-burger place that she remembered had great fries, and pulled in. Will made no movement to get out until Brody climbed out and walked around to his door and opened it for him. Will unfolded his lean body from the vehicle. Brody placed his hand on his shoulder to guide him in, but Will's look of warning made him drop it.

Five minutes later, they were seated at a corner table sipping tea and waiting on their food.

"I realize you don't know me," Brody said. "But I really want to help you, Will."

"My name is Kyle," he said tersely.

Julie gave Brody a sympathetic look, trying to telegraph to him to be patient.

"All right, Kyle." The waitress brought their food and she and Brody dug in. "I think you'll like the horses. At least you used to when you were little."

"How do you know what I liked?" Will asked.

Julie held her breath. She and Brody hadn't discussed when to tell him about the DNA results.

Brody shifted, pushing his fries around on his plate, then shrugged. "Most kids like horses. Especially boys."

Will shrugged. "Whatever."

Brody's jaw tightened in obvious frustration. "Well, we'll see when we get to the BBL."

Kyle didn't respond, but he wolfed down his food as if he hadn't eaten in days.

"You can have another burger if you want," Julie said, wiping ketchup from her mouth with her napkin.

But Will simply folded his napkin neatly and placed it on the table. She noted the meticulous way he handled it and had a sinking feeling his captor had been obsessive-compulsive.

Brody paid the bill, and they drove the rest of the way to the BBL in silence. Cracking through Will's veneer might be harder than she thought.

But getting him to talk was imperative. If his abductor had seen the newscast, he would probably have panicked.

That panic might trigger him to do something bad—like take his anger out on the other kids he was holding.

Or what if he came after Will?

She didn't want to tell Brody, but she'd stick around and keep her eyes peeled. And she'd alert her coworkers.

Will was not only a suspect in a crime and a kidnap victim, but he was also a witness and could identify his abductor.

Which meant he might be in danger.

BRODY WATCHED Will's reaction as they arrived at the BBL, but just as he'd been on the ride and when they'd stopped to buy him some clothes and toiletries, he remained sullen.

Will's look turned even more wary as Brody showed him around the ranch house. He behaved as if he was searching for bars on the window and guards like he was still in prison.

Or maybe that was how it had been where he'd lived the past few years.

"You can have this room," he told Will, strategically giving Julie the first guest room by the stairs and placing Will in the second. Both rooms were situated across from the master suite so he and Julie could monitor if Will left his room and went downstairs.

He also intended to keep the alarm set at night in case Will tried to leave.

Julie set the shopping bag of jeans and shirts in the room, but her phone buzzed and she excused herself to answer it.

"Come on," Brody said. "I'll give you a quick tour of the ranch."

Will's lips pressed into a thin line. "What will my assignments be?"

"Your assignments?" Brody asked.

"Yes, sir. I'm here under court order. I expect to have assignments."

Brody rubbed his chin. He wanted to tell him that his assignment was to remember him, to remember his life before the kidnapping. But he couldn't push. "You mean what will your jobs, your chores be?"

"Sir, yes, sir."

Brody's chest squeezed at the military response. "You can muck stalls, help exercise and groom the horses."

Will's eyes crinkled. "Sir, yes, sir."

"You can stop with that, too," Brody said, his irritation mounting. "This is a camp, not a military base. The boys here call me Brody."

Will's eyebrows lifted slightly. "Sir, yes, sir."

"It's Brody," he said again, struggling for patience. "Now, come on, I'll show you around."

He led Will down the stairs and outside. Julie was on the porch. "I have to go, Brody. I'll be back in a while."

"What's going on?"

She cut her eyes toward Will. "A woman from the fair where Hank Forte went missing called in. She said she saw someone suspicious and is going to meet with a sketch artist."

That sounded hopeful.

"I'll be back in a little bit." She looked at Will. "Anytime you're ready to talk, Kyle, I'm ready to listen."

A mixture of emotions flickered in his eyes for a second, but then his mask fell back into place.

Brody watched her leave, then turned to Will. "My brother and I used to love riding when we were little," he said. "Our father had a spread east of here, not a big one. He wasn't a smart rancher, but we had a couple of horses we used to ride. Chance was mine and my brother, Will, liked this old guy named Tully."

He walked toward the stables where they kept the quarter horses and Will followed. "One day Will took Tully out on the riding trails and Will got turned around. But even though Tully was old, he had a good sense of direction and brought him back." He paused, glancing at Will to see if he had any reaction, but Will seemed to be looking across the land as if he was still searching for the prison guards.

"Another time Tully got spooked when they came up on a skunk. The skunk put out his scent, and when Will rode back, he smelled so bad it took three days to wash the stench off of him." Brody laughed, but Will pulled his chin as if he might be remembering that day.

Brody continued to tell stories about Will as he showed him the horses, then led him to the dining hall. Several of the ranch hands were laughing and talking about a cow that had gotten stuck in the mud, and the campers filled the room with their chatter.

He introduced Will to Carlos, one of the older boys who'd joined them as a counselor after he'd attended the camp, then he spotted Kim Woodstock and Jordan McGregor, counselors and the wives of two of Brody's best friends, and made a mental note to seek their help.

Two of the kids ran up and hugged him, and Brody hugged them back. "How's it going?"

"We roped a calf today," a little guy named Palmer said.

Freddy, an eight-year-old who'd just joined the group this week, grinned. "And Carlos showed us how to play horseshoes."

Brody ruffled the boy's hair. "That was my little brother's favorite game. He used to beat me at it all the time." Actually he'd let Will beat him but the joy on his face had been worth it.

"We're going to camp out under the stars tonight," Palmer said.

"And Carlos said we get to ride with the cattle drive," Freddy exclaimed.

"I'm so proud of both of you." Brody grinned as they raced off.

But when he looked up at Will, his brother was studying him with an odd expression.

"I like seeing the kids so excited," Brody said. "Most of them come from broken homes, and the majority don't have good role models. We teach the kids how to trust, how to have fun and work hard, all about teamwork and respecting themselves and others."

Will lapsed into another sullen silence, but

Brody continued the tour, determined his brother see that the BBL was not a prison. The next few hours he introduced him to a couple of other camp groups. They sat in on the camp out where the kids told stories about what they'd done that day, then they roasted hotdogs over the fire.

Will looked puzzled as they walked from the cookout back to the house. When they reached the porch and Brody sank onto the porch swing, Will hesitated.

"Why did you bring me here?" Will finally asked.

Brody swallowed hard. He didn't know if it was the right moment, but Julie said time was important, that little Hank, and whomever else Will's abductor had, might be in danger.

So he decided to tell him the truth. "Because you're my brother," he said gruffly. "All those stories I told you, they were stories about you and how we grew up."

Will's jaw hardened. "That's not true, my name is Kyle."

Brody met his gaze. "Kyle is the name the man who kidnapped you gave you. Your real name is William Henry Bloodworth." Pain wrenched his chest. "We lived on a small ranch with our father. But we both loved the rodeo and when you were ten years old, we went to a local rodeo."

Will shook his head in denial, but Brody continued. "I was seventeen, your age now. And Julie, Special Agent Whitehead, she was my girlfriend." Brody leaned forward, his breathing labored as the memory haunted him. "Dad had gone to work a job, and I was supposed to watch you. But Julie and I snuck off to the barn to make out, and I left you in the stands alone. When I returned…" his voice cracked and he pinched the bridge of his nose. "You were gone."

"I'm not this Will," he said. "You may want me to be but I'm not. I'm Kyle."

"Yes, you are my brother, Will. The DNA results proved it." Emotions flooded Brody, and he ran his hand through his hair. "I looked for you for years. I dogged the police and FBI, hired private investigators, I told myself I'd never give up. And now you're here." His breath rattled out. "I don't know who took you, but I know he abused you, and…I'm sorry. So sorry that I didn't protect you. So sorry that you've suffered." God, he wanted to pull his brother in his arms and hug him. "I… wish I could change the past, Will, wish I could take back the horrible things that have happened to you, but I can't."

"I'm not this Will," he said, although his voice sounded weak this time, and pain darkened his eyes. "So stop saying I am."

Brody heaved another breath. His chest was about to explode. "Yes, you are." He pulled out a copy of the DNA report he'd received from Julie. "Look at that, Will. It verifies that you are my little brother."

The boy's hands shook as he took the paper and read it. When he glanced back up at Brody, anguish flashed across his features, but denial screamed in his eyes. "No…this is wrong. I wasn't kidnapped. I live with my father and he loves me and…I'm not this Will."

Then he raced inside the house and slammed the door. Brody closed his eyes, praying he hadn't made a mistake by pushing him too hard. Julie said it might take time for Will to come around. To trust him.

But they didn't have time.

Poor little Hank Forte might be getting a beating he didn't deserve right now.

JOSEPHINE CRANTERA fidgeted in the seat beside the TBI sketch artist. "No, he had thick eyebrows. Dark, sort of pinched together."

Julie listened, praying this wasn't a false lead.

"Like this?" Ava, the sketch artist asked as she angled herself so Josephine could see the drawing.

"Yes, yes, that's good. And his nose was flat, like it had been broken. And he had a scar above his right eye."

Julie studied the photo as the woman continued to describe him.

"His face was longer, narrow," Josephine said. "And his eyes, brown. Dark. Beady as if he was up to no good."

"Where was it you saw him?" Julie asked.

"Beside the balloons, you know the dart game."

Julie nodded. "How old was he?"

Josephine twisted her skirt in her hands, bunching it up. "A young man, maybe twenties. But there was something off about him."

"What do you mean?"

"The way he stared at that little boy. It just didn't feel right."

The hairs on the back of Julie's neck prickled. "Go on."

Josephine pressed a hand to her mouth. "It was like he was angry at him, but then he had this strange smile. That's what made me think about him when I saw the picture of the missing little boy on the news."

Julie frowned. The profile of the kidnapper had put him in his twenties when the crimes had just begun, which would make him in his forties now.

Either this woman was wrong, and this young man had nothing to do with Hank Forte's disappearance, or…the kidnapper had a partner in crime.

Josephine squinted at the sketch one more time. "Wait. Something else. He had a birthmark, small but on his neck." She gestured to the right side. "This side, sort of like a strawberry."

Ava added the birthmark then tapped the page. "How is this?"

"Yes, that's good," Josephine said.

Julie's heart hammered as she studied the finished sketch. "Let me have that for a minute."

Ava handed it to her and she rushed to her computer then pulled up the screen shots of all the victims, including the shots showing the age progression.

Dear God.

The sketch of the young man Josephine had seen looked like the first boy who had gone missing twenty years ago.

Jeremy…

He was alive.

Nausea suddenly rose to her throat. He had survived, but judging from Josephine's account, he was now helping his abductor kidnap other boys.

KYLE PACED the room, his pulse racing. He was not Will Bloodworth, that boy Brody Bloodworth talked about. He had never met the man before, never lived on a ranch with him, never ridden a horse named Tully or played horseshoes.

His name was Kyle Wylie. He lived with his father and brothers.

He gave you that name when he took you.

Brody's words taunted him. Father did give his sons new names, names so the people who'd thrown them away wouldn't track them down and hurt them or try to take them away from his family.

But he was not this man's brother.

Why was he trying to make him believe that he was? Why had he brought him here?

Images of the kids running up to Brody and hugging him flashed back. The other campers at the campout had all been smiling and talking to him, too.

All day he'd waited for the prison walls to come down. He'd expected to see barbed wire fencing and guards posted around the ranch. To be punished when he'd arrived.

To go to a dark hole.

But that hadn't happened.

Yet.

What if today was an act to lull him into trusting them?

That TBI agent would be back, too. Back with her questions and probing and demands.

He paced to the window and peeled back the curtain, then stared across the land. No barbed wires or guards. Even the horses ran free and seemed to be treated well.

A fleeting memory tried to shove through the confusion in his head. When Brody had talked about that rodeo…he had seen images of the barrel racers, of calf-roping contests, of a cowboy on a bull.

Those images had seemed real.

But he had never been to a rodeo before.

He closed his eyes, beating his head with his fists. He had to think straight. Think like his father had taught him. As a soldier would.

That TBI agent with the gold hair and tender smile was the enemy. So was Brody Bloodworth with his phony DNA report.

He paced back across the room, then noticed a scrapbook on the table by the bed. Pulse jumping, he picked it up and opened it. A photo of a younger Brody and an older man and a little boy was on the first page. The little boy had sandy-brown hair and freckles and was staring up at Brody as if he was his hero.

That boy must be the Will Brody talked about. The one he thought was him.

The man was confused. He belonged to Father.

Still, curiosity nagged at him, and he flipped the pages. Images of the two brothers together filled his vision. In one picture, Will was about three and was riding on the same horse with Brody. In another when he was a little older, it looked as if Brody was teaching the kid how to ride. Then there were pictures of Brody winning barrel races, of him playing baseball on a high school team. Of Brody teaching Will how to ride a bike.

Then one of the horseshoe game.

His stomach cramped, and Kyle slammed the book shut, then threw it across the room. That had been a happy family.

But it wasn't his and it never would be.

He had to go back to Father. Make sure the other boys weren't being punished because of him.

Footsteps pounded on the steps in the hall, and Will flipped the lights in the room off, kicked off his shoes and crawled into the bed.

He'd wait until Brody was asleep then he'd find a way to escape. He'd seen a Jeep parked beside a truck outside when they'd arrived.

He'd take the vehicle and hightail it back to his father.

Try to save little Hank from the hole.

Footsteps sounded outside the room, and he kept himself locked inside. No way he wanted another confrontation with Brody. Finally sometime after midnight, when the house was dark, he sneaked down the stairs. He wished he had the damn keys to that Jeep, but he could hotwire it in no time.

He held his breath as he slipped out the front door. Like a good soldier escaping the enemy, he didn't make a sound as he closed it. The sky was dark, void of stars, the dark clouds shutting out the light.

It reminded him of the hole.

Father might put him back there when he returned, but he'd have to risk it. His boots snapped twigs as he crossed to the vehicle, the sound of a horse whinnying in the distance making him pause.

But he didn't have time to dwell on it. He had to escape.

He scanned the area around the Jeep and the pastures but didn't see anyone, so he eased open the door to the Jeep, then slid in and bent over to try to hotwire the vehicle.

Suddenly footsteps crunched gravel, echoing in the silence, and he realized someone had seen him. His heart raced. He had to hurry.

A figure suddenly appeared behind him. He felt it, heard his breathing. He gritted his teeth, fear immobilizing him.

It was too late to escape. Too late to help little Hank.

Chapter Eleven

Brody fought disappointment as he grabbed the car door. He'd hoped he'd gotten through to Will earlier, maybe triggered some memories, but apparently not.

The boy would rather go back to his abuser than stay with him.

That hurt.

"If you need to go somewhere, I'll be glad to drive you," he said.

Will spun around toward him, his eyes wild with fright. Brody's pulse clamored as he realized that Will was afraid of him.

Or maybe he'd thought he was someone else?

Will wrapped his hands around the steering wheel with a white-knuckled grip. "You'd take me?" he asked.

Brody grimaced at the scars on his knuckles. "That depends on where you were going. You want to take me to the man who kidnapped you and Hank?"

Will glared at him. "No."

"Then like it or not, you're under my supervision. It's here or back to jail."

"Like this isn't another prison?" Will asked in a sharp voice.

Brody sighed. "Does this ranch look like a prison? Are there bars on your windows? Guards at the door? Cells?"

Will gave him a challenging look. "You picked up troubled kids from orphanages and brought them here to work for you. You may act nice at first, but I bet once you have them here for a while, all that changes."

"Is that what happened to you?" Brody asked. "The man who kidnapped you treated you nice at first, then he turned on you and started beating you?"

The color drained from Will's face, and he averted his eyes as if he realized he'd said too much.

"He beat you and locked you up and did God knows what?" Brody said, the images haunting him. "So why would you go back to him?" He pounded his fist on the roof of the car. "That is where you were going, isn't it?"

Will worked his mouth from side to side, then slid from the car and faced him. "You wouldn't understand if I told you."

"Try me." Brody squared his shoulders. Will

was almost as tall as him but leaner. Still he had that hardness in his eyes that cut him to the bone.

Will made a sarcastic sound low in his throat. "Why? So you can use it against me?"

Brody silently cursed. "You've got it all wrong, Will. I'm on your side just like I am for these kids. I don't bring them here to work. I don't beat them or hurt them. Most of them have had some hard knocks in their lives. They've been abused, abandoned, hurt, and some of them have even skirted trouble with the law." He paused to let that sink in. "But I treat them with respect, teach them to respect themselves. No one on my staff, and that includes me, ever lays a hand to one of them in anger."

Brody gave him an imploring look. "Please, let me help you. Talk to me."

"You can't help me," Will said, his voice low, filled with despair. "No one can."

Brody reached out to touch him, but Will jerked away.

Headlights suddenly beamed a path down the drive, and Brody sighed in relief again. He'd been waiting up on Julie, wondering why she'd been gone so long.

But when she rolled to a stop and climbed out, the expression on her face sent tension coiling in his belly.

She shot a look at Will. "We have to talk."

Brody gritted his teeth. Something was wrong. Was Will in more trouble than he thought?

JULIE DREADED the conversation she was about to have because of Brody. But she had to question Will again.

And push him harder to tell the truth.

The realization that Brody and Will had been having an altercation beside the Jeep hit her.

She narrowed her eyes at Will. "What's going on out here?"

Will clamped his mouth shut and stared across the pasture. Brody shrugged. "We were just talking."

Will glanced at Brody as if he was surprised he hadn't revealed more. Judging from the fact that they were standing beside the SUV, she'd bet Will had tried to escape.

She pointed toward the house. "Let's go inside."

Brody gestured to Will, and Julie led the way into the house, then veered into Brody's office.

"What's wrong?" Brody asked as she set her briefcase on the conference table Brody used for meetings.

Julie cut her eyes toward Will, then removed a folder and opened it. "Sit down, Will, I have some questions for you."

All emotion fled from his face, and he resumed his military mask as he slid into the wooden chair.

Brody looked nervous, but Julie forced herself to focus.

Julie wanted the man who'd taken Will, and she was going to find him, even if it hurt Will and Brody in the process.

She laid Hank Forte's photograph on the table and pushed it toward Will. "Do you recognize this little boy?"

A muscle ticked in Will's jaw. "I already told you I don't."

"The thing is, Will, I know you're lying."

He stiffened and shot her a cold look.

"See," Julie continued. "I think that the same man who kidnapped you seven years ago kidnapped him."

Will folded his arms.

"I also think that he kidnapped all of these kids." She pushed photo after photo onto the table, forcing him to look at them. Then she tapped Jeremy's photo. "We believe that this boy was his first victim."

Then she laid the drawing the sketch artist had created from the woman's testimony in front of Will. "You say you don't know these other boys. But this guy—how about him?"

Will's eyes flickered but he didn't speak.

"We have special software programs at the FBI that take photographs of missing children and show their age progression," Julie said. "Periodically we post these on the National Center for Missing and Exploited Children. These photographs stay in our databases because we never stop looking for the children."

"Julie?" Brody asked.

She threw up a hand to silence him, then placed Jeremy's childhood photo beside the sketch again. "You didn't know this little boy because he was kidnapped before you. By the time you were abducted, he had been brainwashed."

Will blew air between his teeth. He was putting on an I-don't-give-a-damn look, but she also read nervous signs. Beneath the table his leg had started to jiggle.

"Maybe you consider Jeremy your brother," Julie said. "But he was a victim just like you. And just like little Hank Forte." She touched his picture again, and Will's mouth went flat.

"All this time we've assumed that the kidnapper was in his twenties when he started, so now he would be in his forties." She tucked a strand of hair behind her ear. "But now I'm wondering if he has a partner."

Brody leaned over the pictures and studied the sketch of Jeremy. "What are you saying?"

"I just met with a woman who saw a suspicious young man at the local fair where Hank went missing. She said that he was watching Hank while he played the dart-balloon game."

Will's face looked tormented, the first sign of real emotion.

"She described the young man to our sketch artist and this is what he looked like." She waved it in front of Will. "Do you recognize him, Will?"

"My name is Kyle," Will choked out.

"No, it's not," Julie said sternly. "It's Will Bloodworth, and this man Brody is your brother. But you consider Jeremy your brother, don't you?" She stood. "Is that why you're protecting him?" Her voice rose, grew harsh. "Because it looks like Jeremy is helping the man you call your father, and he helped lure Hank Forte away from his parents. It looks like Jeremy helped abduct Hank."

Brody hissed, anguish in his expression, but Julie continued.

"Did you help him kidnap this little boy, too, Will? Is that the reason you won't talk? The man you call father taught you and Jeremy to do his dirty work for him."

Will shot up. "I didn't help him take that boy!"

Brody gripped the edge of the table. He started to speak, but Julie shook her head at him, warning him to let her handle the questioning.

"Jeremy did, though," Julie said, her heart pounding. "Jeremy was kidnapped when he was a little boy and brainwashed to the point that now he's aiding in more abductions. And the fact that you're covering for him—"

"I'm not covering for him," Will bellowed.

Julie slammed her hands on the table. "Yes, you are, Will. By keeping quiet and protecting the man who took you, you are covering for him." She swept her hand across the pictures. "You're helping him hurt these other kids. Tell me, what does he do to them? Beat them? Lock them up in a dark room? Starve them until they beg for food and water?" She heaved a breath. "What is he doing to little Hank right now? Hank is probably terrified, crying for his mother and father. What does the man you call Father do when he cries, Will?"

"Stop it!" Will hissed.

"No, I won't stop," Julie said. "I won't stop until I find this little boy and take him home to his mother and father. I won't stop until I save him from becoming like Jeremy."

Pain wrenched Will's face. Brody reached out to touch him, but Will backed away.

"Please, Will, tell us where this man kept you," Brody said. "Where is he holding Hank?"

But Will refused to answer. Instead, he adopted his sullen, closed expression again. "I don't know. Now if you're finished, I'll go back to my cell."

"Your room is not a cell," Brody snapped. "This is your home, Will.

"I want you to help us find that little boy and the other missing kids, so we can get these charges dropped against you and you can come here to live. So you can have the life you should have had." Brody's voice cracked. "The life that that monster stole from you." He took Will's arm and forced him to look at him. "I love you. You're my brother and I want you back here where you belong."

Will's gaze met his for a moment, emotions tingeing his eyes as if he wanted to believe what Brody was saying.

But he couldn't. That was evident when he pulled away and backed toward the door.

"Think about what your brother said," Julie said quietly. "Help us find Hank and the other boys so they can go back to their families and have a normal life."

He hesitated, his expression tormented, but a second later, he darted out the door. His footsteps pounded on the steps, then the sound of his door closing echoed through the house.

Julie knotted her hands in frustration, but Brody strode to the bar in the corner of his office, poured himself a shot of whiskey, then tossed it down. When he turned back to her, the anguish in his eyes made her heart ache.

She couldn't get involved with Brody again, couldn't allow herself to get close.

But she also couldn't stand still when he was in such agony.

So she went to him and did what she'd wanted to do since the first moment she'd seen him again.

She pulled him in her arms.

BRODY'S BODY SHOOK as Julie wrapped her arms around him. He didn't know how to feel or think. Julie had been rough on Will, but he understood her reason.

God…were the things she'd said true? Had Jeremy, one of the victims of this monster, helped abduct Hank Forte?

"I'm sorry, Brody," Julie murmured. "I know you're upset, that that was difficult."

He closed his eyes, inhaled a deep breath, savoring the comfort she offered. "You think Will really helped kidnap that little boy?"

Julie's labored sigh echoed in the tense silence. "I don't know, Brody." She rubbed his arms with her hands. "I want to say that he didn't."

"But he did rob those stores," Brody said gruffly.

"Yes," Julie admitted. "But even if he did help lure Hank away, he was probably forced to do so. So was Jeremy. We know Jeremy and Will were both abused, both physically and mentally. It's going to take time to learn the details of what happened to them."

"I know. Earlier I caught Will trying to steal that Jeep."

"I figured that was what happened."

"He accused me of being like his kidnapper, of bringing the kids here to the BBL to force them to work." His throat grew thick. "He said I was probably nice to them at first, then I turned on them."

Julie's chest squeezed, and she reached up and stroked his jaw. "Obviously that's all he's ever known. Right now, he doesn't trust anyone. Give him time, he'll realize that you're nothing like that monster who kidnapped him."

Brody prayed she was right.

Then Julie's finger brushed his jaw, and the tension in his body coiled tighter. Only this kind of tension came from the realization that she was in his arms, that her breasts were pressed against his chest, that her lips were only a hairbreadth away from his own.

He'd thought about her so many times over the years. Had wanted her so much. Had dreamt about this moment.

"Brody, I'm so sorry," Julie whispered. "But I will make this right."

He gently brushed her hair from her forehead, the silky tendrils driving him crazy with lust.

"You've already done a lot," he murmured. Then he lowered his head and closed his lips over hers. She moaned and parted her lips, and Brody dragged her closer, deepening the kiss.

God, he wanted her. He always had.

He always would.

JULIE LOST HERSELF in the kiss. She'd craved Brody for so long that it was all she could do not to beg him to make love to her.

His hands threaded through her hair, tangling in the long tresses, reminding her of how he'd loved to play with it when they were younger.

The way it felt as he yanked her closer just before he lost control and thrust inside her.

She reached for his shirt, hungry to touch his bare skin, to feel the rough coarse hair on his broad chest.

To kiss his neck and torso and trail her tongue down to his sex.

Her hands grew frenzied, pulling at his shirt, and he lowered his head and nipped at her neck, then lower to suckle her breasts through her shirt.

But a noise suddenly made them both jerk apart. Will inside his room.

He was pacing, murmuring something she couldn't understand.

Her breath rasped out in spurts as she tried to regain control. Brody ran his hands over her shoulders where he'd parted her blouse, his eyes smoky as he tilted her face toward him with his thumb.

"We can't do this, Julie."

Hurt suffused her and she pulled away, straightening her clothes. "Why? Because you still blame me? Because I was too rough on your brother?"

Brody dragged her back to him, his eyes smokier than she'd ever seen them. Hunger and need flared in his expression, his breathing as ragged as her own.

"No," he said between clenched teeth. "I meant we can't do it now." His gaze dropped to her breasts, and her body tingled, her nipples stiffening to turgid aching peaks.

"But we will make love," he said. "I will have you again, because I've never stopped wanting you."

Julie's heart stuttered, a myriad of emotions flooding her throat so she couldn't speak.

"Now go to bed before I change my mind and take you right here in the hall." He gestured toward Will's room. "And we both know that's not a good idea."

Julie nodded in concession, although she wanted to tell him that she didn't care. She was tired of work, tired of hunting down sadistic killers, tired of seeing women's bloody bodies in her sleep, and tortured little boys crying out for help while she was awake.

But she knew he was right.

Still, his words taunted her as she rushed into the guest room and shut the door.

She started to undress, and her hand slid over her gun. She'd vowed to find Brody's brother and bring him back to him, but he didn't really have him back yet.

She wouldn't give up until she did.

Then and only then could she believe that she might have a chance with Brody.

KYLE STARED AT the photo of Brody and the kid on the wall, then at the photo album, his stomach churning. Images were starting to claw at his mind.

Images of skipping rocks in a creek, of another guy there with him showing him how to angle them just right.

Of Brody.

Brody showing him how to saddle a horse. How to rope a calf. How to throw horseshoes.

No…he had never lived on a ranch. Brody was playing with his head. He'd doctored that DNA report because he wanted him to believe that he was his brother.

They were trying to trick him into ratting out Father. Father had said that the police were like that, that they were the enemy. That they would lie to him, beat him, try to make him believe things that weren't true.

His home was back with Father and Jeremy and the others.

He closed his eyes, willing the images he'd seen today to leave his mind. They hadn't been real.

Except those boys had been laughing at the campout. Talking and having fun.

Fun…not allowed at the compound.

Then he saw Hank's face. Hank crying as Jeremy had brought him to Father. Father's harsh look as he'd dragged Hank to the pit.

Hank's scream as he was closed into the darkness.

He began to shake, sweat beading on his skin. He was back there again, back in the hole, the cold dark swallowing him. He tried to count the minutes until Father would return, but minutes turned into hours. Hours into days.

Days he couldn't remember because the terror had played with his mind.

That agent Julie thought he'd helped lure Hank to Father. That made his stomach roil. He hadn't lured Hank.

But still Hank was there now. Suffering. Terrified. Alone.

Brody's words echoed in his head. *I love you, Will. I want to help you.*

Father had said he loved him, too. Just before he'd whipped him.

Just before he'd closed him in the pit.

He went to the door. Maybe he should tell that agent…no.

The only way to save Hank was for him to go back.

He paced and paced, then finally decided he'd better turn off the light and pretend to be asleep or that agent and Brody might be suspicious. So he settled on the bed, but that stupid photo album called to him, and he opened it up and studied the pictures again.

The little boy with the sandy blond hair had looked happy. He was learning to tie a rope in one picture. In another, Brody was teaching him how to saddle a horse. In another, they were out on the boat in the lake fishing.

He slammed the book shut. That little boy wasn't him.

He'd never smiled like that or tied a rope or saddled a horse or gone fishing.

They were all lies Brody had told him.

He had to escape.

But not tonight. He'd already been caught once. He'd have to lay low. Play it like a good soldier. Wait for the right moment.

An hour later, the house was dark and quiet, and he was actually nodding off when he suddenly saw something flickering through the sheer curtains. He stood and went to look out the window to see if it was a car's headlights.

But his pulse hammered when he saw it was a fire.

The barn across the way was in flames.

And the horses were inside.

Chapter Twelve

Brody jumped from his bed at the sound of the pounding on the door. He swung it open and saw Will in the hallway, his eyes panicked.

"A fire…the barn…I saw it through my window," Will cried.

Brody raced to Will's room, pushed back the sheers and saw the flames shooting up toward the sky. Pure rage shot through him. Dammit, the horses were trapped in there.

"Call 9-1-1, get a fire truck out here now!" Brody yelled.

He ran back to his room, yanked on a T-shirt, jeans, socks and boots. By the time he was dressed, Julie was at the door, her hair spiraling out of control, her hands twisting at her T-shirt and pajama pants.

"What's wrong?"

"The barn's on fire," Brody said. "I have to get the horses out."

"I'm coming, too." She darted into her room,

and he raced down the stairs. Footsteps pounded behind him and he realized Will was on his tail.

Brody had grabbed his phone and punched his foreman's number, cursing as he waited on it to ring. Curtis was new and younger than his former foreman. He just hoped he was half as good.

Finally he answered. "The barn's on fire. Send some men out to help."

"We'll be there ASAP," Curtis said.

"What do we do?" Will asked as he chased Brody outside.

"We have to get the horses out!" Brody ran toward the barn, half panicked at the sight of the smoke billowing in a thick cloud.

Julie caught up with them as he yanked open the barn door. "How many horses?"

"Four," Brody shouted over the roar of the flames. The fire looked as if it had started in the tack room and was probably spreading back toward the stalls. It would take only minutes to eat up the wood and hay and the barn would be gone.

Heat radiated off the building and made it nearly impossible to breathe, but Brody yanked a handkerchief over his mouth and raced in.

"Stay here, and wait for the ambulance," he yelled at Julie and Will as he dashed into the barn.

Flames spiked around him in patches, the tack room nearly fully engulfed. He coughed as the smoke filled his lungs, then raced to the first stall, dodging flames and falling wood as the section that had caught the roof sent boards crackling and flying down.

Behind him, he realized Julie had followed and so had Will.

"Get the two on the end out," he said, knowing their stalls were the farthest from the raging fire.

Julie ran past him and so did Will, both coughing and dodging the splintered boards falling from the roof.

The horses were terrified, banging against the stalls, kicking and pounding to escape. Brody touched the latch on the first stall, the heat scalding his face and fingers as he turned the latch. "Come on, Sassy, get out of here."

The terrified animal rose and kicked at him, but he lowered his voice to a soothing voice. "Come on, get out of here, girl."

He slid into the stall, then slapped the horse's hind section, and she shot forward, whinnying as she ran toward the back.

Flames inched toward the second stall, the smoke so thick and gray that his vision blurred, and he bent over to draw a breath.

One breath and he reached for the latch. It was hot, the flames starting to eat the floor of the horse's stall. She was going crazy, whinnying, kicking and slamming her hoofs against the barn wall.

"Come on, Honey," he said softly. "I know it's bad, but we have to leave the barn."

She rose on her back legs and kicked at him, but he held up a hand. "It's me, girl. Come on, it's hot in here."

She bawled and kicked though, and Brody knew she wasn't going to come willingly. He looked back at the tack room but it was completely gone. Flames crawled toward him at a sickening pace, wood splintering and crackling all around him.

"Brody?" Julie cried. "Are you in here?"

"Yes, get Will and get out!" he shouted.

"He's safe," she shouted. "And the other horses are outside."

"I'll be right there!" he yelled. "Go on!"

He spotted a rope in the next stall, then grabbed it and raced back to Honey. She was out of control, bucking and kicking but the flames were about to reach her hoofs.

He made a looped knot and threw it around her neck. She bucked as he tightened it, and he had to brace his feet while she fought. "Come on, girl, I'm trying to save you, help me out."

He pulled and yanked and talked in a low tone until finally he coaxed her out. The moment she left the stall, he let loose the rope and slapped her behind. "Go on, girl, get out of here!"

She galloped out of the barn, flaming boards falling around them as he chased her outside. By the time he exited the barn, the smoke had grown so thick he could hardly see. But the wail of the fire truck rent the air, and Julie's hands touched his face.

"We got them all out," she said as he fell to the ground, coughing and begging for air.

"Will?"

"He helped," Julie said.

Then they both scanned the area, but Will was nowhere in sight.

Dammit. He had disappeared.

JULIE HEAVED FOR a breath as the smoke billowed higher in the sky. Three ranch hands had arrived, yanking a hose from the house and trying to douse the flames.

The siren wailed closer, the fire truck screeching to a stop, workers jumping down and rolling out their hoses to attack the fire. Heat wafted off the barn, flames shooting toward the sky, wood splintering and cracking as the barn began to crumble.

Brody jogged over to meet the firemen. "The horses are all safe, and the barn's lost. Just try to keep it from spreading."

"How did it start?" the lead fireman asked.

"I don't know but look for the origin," Brody said. "I have to find my brother."

Julie's pulse clamored as she scanned the area. "The Jeep's still here and so is the truck."

Brody scowled. "I'll check the other side of the barn." He ran to the right then behind the flaming building, and Julie hurried to check the house.

"Will! Are you in here?" She dashed through the house, checking the office, then the bedrooms but the bag of clothes she'd bought Will still lay on the bed unopened.

She snatched her service revolver and phone from her room and strapped it on, then jogged back down the steps. By the time she made it back outside, the barn collapsed with a thunderous roar.

The scene was chaos as the firemen and ranch hands worked to extinguish it. She squinted through the smoke, searching for Brody and Will. Then she spotted two figures running toward the wooded area to the west.

Brody raced from the back of the burning barn, sweat and soot coating his skin.

"Brody!" She motioned him to head west, and she took off running.

He met her at the corner of the stable. "I saw two figures running that way." She pointed toward the woods, and Brody headed into the thicket of trees.

Twigs and leaves snapped, the sound of the blaze echoing in the air as they ran deeper into the woods. Julie saw the figures veer to the right, and she took a shortcut, praying she could catch them.

Although she'd had training and jogged regularly to stay in shape, Brody's legs were longer and he sprinted ahead of her.

"Will, stop!" Brody shouted.

Julie shoved a strand of hair behind her ear, perspiration trickling down the back of her neck as she tried to keep up. A branch slapped her in the face, but she shoved it away, ignoring her stinging cheek, then she jumped over a stump.

By the time she reached the clearing, Brody was leaning against a tree, anger coloring his face. Dust spewed from the back of an old pickup truck in the distance, blurring her vision. She had a bad feeling Will was in that truck.

And that he was getting away.

She stumbled forward and gripped the tree, her chest aching for air.

"Did you see him?" she wheezed.

Pain wrenched Brody's face as he cut his eyes toward her. Then he gave a clipped nod and wiped sweat from his face. "Jeremy was with him," he said through gritted teeth.

"Good God," Julie said. "I wonder if he set that fire as a diversion to get Will."

BRODY CLENCHED HIS HANDS into fists. Had Jeremy set the fire?

Maybe he and Will planned his escape together. But how would they have made contact?

He had to clear his throat to force the words out. "You think Will set it to get away?"

Julie reached for her phone. "Don't go there, Brody. He was the one who woke you up to tell you about the fire, remember? He helped save the horses."

Brody's chest eased slightly. "So why would he go back with Jeremy, especially after all the things we told him?"

"I don't know. He's scared. That family, that life, it's all he knows." She tried her phone but there was no connection. "Let's go back. I have to call this in."

Panic seized Brody, and he caught her by the arm. "Julie, what if some cop chases them down and shoots Will?"

Julie's eyes crinkled with concern as she squeezed his hand. "They'll have orders not to shoot unless it's in self-defense. But you know I can't hide the fact that he left the ranch, Brody. Will and Jeremy both know where Hank Forte is. We have to find them."

He didn't like it, but he knew she was right. He wanted Will found, wanted to know why he'd run from the brother who loved him to the man who'd abused him for years.

God, he'd hoped that when Will saw the family photos and heard stories about their youth he'd remember his life before the kidnapping.

But he hadn't, and now he'd lost him again.

"Come on." They walked back through the woods, the sight of the smoke still billowing above the pasture making anger knot in his belly.

"At least no one was hurt and the horses are okay," Julie said as they reached the pasture.

"But the animals could have died, and someone could have been hurt," Brody said. "*You* could have been hurt, Julie."

Julie's expression softened as if she was touched by his concern. "I'm fine and so are you. We'll find Will again, I promise."

Brody wanted to believe her, but if Will told Jeremy the feds were looking for him, he'd probably run.

The bastard had been hiding out for twenty years and hadn't been caught. He could hide out another twenty and they might never know where he was.

And little Hank Forte might grow up like Will and forget about his real family.

The next two hours were chaos as the firefighters worked to extinguish the last flames. The barn was lost, but he called the vet to check the horses, and Sheriff McRae had arrived and alerted the locals to look for the truck.

"I called the bureau," Julie said. "They're alerting local authorities and issuing an APB on Will and Jeremy. They will put one out on Jeremy. Sadly his parents died a while back."

Brody scrubbed a sweaty hand through his hair. "Maybe it's for the best. It would be hell to finally find your son and learn that he's wanted by the FBI for aiding his kidnapper."

Julie stroked his arm. "Maybe there's hope for him," Julie said. "And don't give up on Will. We have no idea what's going on in his head. Maybe on some level he did remember you."

Brody sighed. Dr. Hornsby, the middle-aged vet with graying hair, approached, his hands in his lab coat. "The horses are okay," he said. "I didn't detect any signs of smoke inhalation."

Brody shook his hand. "Thanks, Doc, that's a relief."

David Thornton, the fire investigator, had also arrived, and had been examining the scene. Brody saw him talking to Sheriff McRae and strode over to them. "Did you find something?"

Thornton gestured toward a gas can lying near a shovel in the rubble. "Looks like someone set it on purpose." He folded his arms. "You have yourself an enemy, Bloodworth? Or do you think it was one of the kids on the ranch?"

"I know who it was," Brody said, his throat thick. "And I know why he set it."

Sheriff McRae adjusted his Stetson. "I'll let you know if we get a hit on that truck."

Brody thanked him then explained the situation to the fire investigator.

Julie had been speaking with one of the ranch hands, but she darted over. "Brody, I have to go."

"Did someone find Will and Jeremy?"

"Not yet," Julie said, her look full of compassion. "But Chief Hurt said a detective in San Antonio arrested another teenager in a convenience store robbery. They took the boy's prints, and it turns out he's one of our missing kids."

"I'm going with you."

Julie shook her head. "You have your hands full here. I'll call you."

"No," Brody said. "I'm going. The sheriff and my ranch hands can take care of what needs to be done here."

Julie hesitated, but finally shrugged. "Let me get my keys."

"No, I'll drive," Brody said. "Just give me a minute." He stepped back to talk to the sheriff for a moment, then hurried inside and snatched his keys.

A minute later, they climbed in his Jeep and headed off the ranch. The smoke curling in the sky behind him taunted him with what had happened tonight, and despair threatened. He wondered if he had lost his brother forever this time.

Still, hope fought its way through. Will hadn't talked, but maybe this kid would. Then they could track down the bastard who'd kidnapped him and lock him away for good.

KYLE COULD STILL smell the smoke on his clothes and hear the horses bawling to escape. Sweat cloaked his body as he remembered the frantic scene, the flames erupting, ceiling falling, the heat sucking the breath from him.

Then Jeremy had appeared, and he'd realized that he had set the fire.

The truck barreled over the ruts in the road. Face flushed with anger, Jeremy suddenly swung the truck onto a side road, racing onto the dirt road and flying into a desolate area that looked as if it went nowhere. A ravine appeared ahead, and fear shot through him.

Jeremy whipped the truck near the edge, parked and jerked around to him. One hand snatched Kyle by the shirt collar, yanking it so tightly he was nearly choking him.

"You stupid fool," Jeremy said in a sinister voice. "What did you tell them?"

"Nothing," Kyle said, his throat raw.

"Nothing?" Jeremy snarled. "You've been with that agent and came here to live with that rancher, and you didn't tell them anything about the family? About where we live? About the compound and Father and the brotherhood?"

"No, I didn't, I swear it," Kyle said shakily. "But

Jeremy, they said that Father took us from our families, that you were the first one he kidnapped."

Jeremy's eyes widened. "Shut up, Kyle. The law lies to people, to kids," he said. "Father told you they were bad, that they invade people's privacy. They locked you up, didn't they?"

"Yes, but I didn't talk."

"Not even when they beat you?"

"They didn't beat me," Kyle said. "They just asked me questions."

"You told them about Father?"

"I told you I didn't tell them anything…."

"What about Hank?"

His stomach roiled. "No. Nothing."

"You know Hank's parents didn't want him. That Father is taking him in to make a man out of him. That his parents paid Father to take him."

Kyle nodded. Although Brody's words echoed in his head. Father had told him that his other daddy didn't want him, either. That his brother wanted to get rid of him.

But Brody said they'd looked for him for years. That he…loved him.

That his real name was Will Bloodworth. That he was that little sandy-haired boy smiling in those pictures.

But Jeremy's fury made him hold his tongue.

Jeremy hated anyone who came between him and Father. Anyone who crossed him.

Was he going to kill him now, then dump his body into the ravine where no one would ever find him?

Chapter Thirteen

Brody tried to focus on the road as they drove toward San Antonio. "Who was the kid they caught?"

"Tray Goodner. Apparently he tried a robbery on his own and the owner retaliated. Took a shot at him and skimmed his arm. Nothing serious but we're meeting Chief Hurt at the hospital."

"This is unreal," Brody said his hands sweating. "How in the hell do you deal with this kind of stress all the time?"

Julie sighed tiredly and rubbed at a knot in her shoulder. "I wanted to find Will."

Brody glanced at her, his heart in his throat. "I'm so sorry for the way I acted years ago. I was hurting and looking for someone to blame because I knew Will's disappearance was my fault."

"Forget it, Brody," Julie said. "I've dealt with enough cases to see how people react during trauma. People either pull together or the trauma drives them apart."

He grimaced. He should have clung to Julie

back then, realized that he could lose her any minute just as he'd lost his brother. Instead, he'd blamed her and driven her to this dark world.

"Do you actually like the job?" he asked. "I mean, how could you?"

"It was challenging at first," Julie said quietly. "But I felt like I was helping people, somehow making up for what I'd done wrong."

Brody cradled her hand in his. "You didn't do anything wrong, Julie. Like you told me, we were kids, teenagers doing what all teenagers do."

"I know, but still, Will was hurt because of it. We have to save him."

The fear lacing her voice told him she'd seen more unhappy endings to her cases than happy ones.

"When this is over, are you thinking about doing something else?"

Julie licked her lips. "I don't know, Brody. I… am tired. I worked that Slasher case. It still haunts me at night."

Dear God. The case where the women had been butchered, their reproductive organs cut out. "I can't believe you saw that. It must have been horrible."

"It was," Julie admitted. "But no more horrible than some of the things I've seen humans do to children."

Brody swallowed hard, her words making his fear rise.

"I'm sorry," she whispered in a pained voice. "I'm supposed to be optimistic, professional, encourage you."

"You have. I thought I'd never see Will again, but now I know he's alive, and we won't stop until he's safe." Brody squeezed her hand again and held it tightly against his thigh as he maneuvered the Jeep into the hospital parking lot. He had thrust her into this world of horrors and he was terrified of what he might hear from the kid they'd caught.

But this time he didn't intend to drive Julie away. He needed her.

And he sensed she needed him, too.

JULIE FLASHED HER BADGE at the police officer outside Tray Goodner's door. Apparently the doctor had removed the bullet and the injury wasn't serious, but the thirteen-year-old was dehydrated and had bruises covering his body that garnered suspicion.

Unfortunately Julie knew where he had gotten them.

She tapped on the door, then she and Brody entered. The boy was sleeping, his body a small lump in the hospital bed. According to her information, Tray was eight when he disappeared, making him thirteen now. But he was so thin and haggard-looking that he looked around eleven or twelve. Dark bags shadowed his eyes, indicating he was probably malnourished.

An IV dripped fluids into his body and his right arm was bandaged. He looked dirty, his hair chopped off in uneven layers.

She glanced at Brody and saw the turmoil in his eyes. "You can wait outside if you want," she whispered.

"Stop treating me like I can't handle it," he said gruffly. "This is the reason I started the BBL."

"I'M SORRY," Julie said in a low voice. "I didn't mean it like that." She simply wanted to protect him.

He squeezed her arm. "I know. Now let's do this together."

Julie crossed the room to the bed, hesitated beside it, then brushed the boy's dirty blond hair back. She didn't want to think about the horrible things that had happened to him.

"Tray?"

He slowly opened his eyes, blue eyes that looked frightened.

"Tray, my name is Julie. I work with the TBI."

His thin lips pinched together.

"That is your name isn't it? Tray?"

He shook his head. "RJ."

Julie choked back her anger. "Okay, RJ. How are you feeling? Does your arm hurt?"

His eye twitched. "It's no big deal."

He'd probably had worse. "You're going to be all right," Julie said softly. "But you are in trouble, RJ."

He cut his eyes away from her.

"RJ, I know that whoever you live with made you do this. We have you on camera with Kyle robbing those first stores." She paused. "Kyle was in our custody for a while, but he disappeared tonight with Jeremy."

RJ jerked his head back toward her, his eye twitching again, and Julie dragged a chair up beside his bed. "This man is Brody Bloodworth. He's a rancher who owns a place called the BBL."

RJ looked up at Brody who moved up beside her. "Hey there, RJ."

Julie offered the kid a small smile. "I know you're scared—"

"I'm not scared of anything," RJ said quickly.

Julie gave a small nod. "All right, you're a tough guy. But you're also in a bad situation. I can help you though."

"I don't need no help."

"Yes, you do," Julie said matter-of-factly. "So I'm going to tell you everything we know, then let you fill in the blanks."

RJ shrugged as if he knew he had no recourse.

"Brody is here because his little brother was kidnapped seven years ago. When we caught Kyle, we took his DNA and discovered he's Brody's little brother. We also believe that you were stolen from your family, RJ." She paused, but noted his eye twitching faster. "We have software that shows age progression for missing children, and our program tells me that your real name is Tray Goodner."

He twisted the sheets with his uninjured hand.

"Your mother reported you missing from a carnival." She touched his hand. "Your mother is still alive and misses you very much, Tray. She's been looking for you all these years and loves you."

"That's not true," Tray hissed. "She sold me. That's how Father got all of us. He saved us from the people who threw us away."

Brody flinched beside her, and she let him speak. "That's not true," Brody said. "I love my brother and want him back. I know your mother feels the same way."

Julie removed the photographs from her bag and held them up one by one. "Jeremy was the first boy we believe this man, your father, kidnapped. He started twenty years ago."

Fear drew the muscles in RJ's face. "Next came this boy, Carl Fanning, then Daryl Derwin, Anthony Putnam and after that Jeff Wickman." She flashed the photo from when they were taken then the age progression sketch, watching for Tray's reaction. He gripped the sheet tighter with each sketch she showed. "Next he took Phil Jasper, then Will Bloodworth, then five years ago, you joined his family."

Anguish blended with fear in Tray's eyes, and he made a small sound in his throat.

"Two years ago he added Lewis Renz, and just a few days ago, he took six-year-old Hank Forte."

Tray's face paled at the sight of Hank's photograph.

"His parents have been all over the news begging people to help them find their son."

"We know he beats you, abuses you," Brody interjected. "Maybe he brainwashes you, and that little Hank is suffering now. He's terrified and wants his mother and father just like you did five years ago."

Julie showed him a picture of Hank's parents. "These are the Fortes. They are devastated over their son's disappearance, just like your mother was." Then she removed another picture from her stash and held it up in front of him. "This is your mother, Tray. She loves you and has never given up looking for you. She wants you back just like Hank's parents want him back."

Emotions suddenly flooded Tray's face. "He told us our parents sold us, that they didn't want us."

"He lied to you," Julie said giving his hand another squeeze. "He told you those things to make you trust him, to make you depend on him. He wanted you to believe that so you wouldn't try to escape."

"He locked us up," Tray admitted, his voice cracking. "He... If we didn't obey he punished us. When Kyle got caught, he...beat all of us."

Brody cleared his throat. "He's a bad man," he said in a gruff tone. "Tell us where to find him, and we can get all the boys back with their families."

"How many boys live with your father now?" Julie asked.

Tray sniffled, wiping at his eyes with his uninjured hand. "Five."

Five. But there were ten missing... "So he has Jeremy, Will, you and Hank?"

"I didn't count Jeremy cause he...he helps him."

Julie's throat constricted. So she'd been right. "He helped lure Hank to your father?"

Tray gave a small wary nod. "And Renny."

Julie narrowed her eyes then showed him the pictures. "Which one is Renny?"

His finger shook as he pointed to the photo of Lewis Renz.

"There's one more," Julie said. She laid out the photos. "Who else is with him?"

He pointed to the picture of Phil Jasper.

Brody released a pent up breath. "What happened to the others?"

Tray gripped the sheet into a knot and looked down, his body trembling. "He got rid of them."

Julie clenched her hands into balls. "What do you mean?"

Tray closed his eyes. "They disappear," he whispered in a haunted voice. "And they don't come back."

BRODY'S BLOOD TURNED to ice, his worst fears confirmed. This monster killed the boys who didn't cooperate. Or he killed some of them just to make a point.

What would he do to Will when he went back? And why would Will go back if he knew that the man might kill him?

"Will's going back to save the others, not because he's loyal to this man," Brody said, the truth dawning. "Is that right, Tray?"

Tray shrugged. "I don't know."

"Is he protective of the others, or does he help this man you call Father kidnap other boys?"

Tray rubbed at the bandage on his arm. "He doesn't help like Jeremy," he said. "Kyle…I've seen him take a beating so the little ones don't have to."

Emotions flooded Brody. In spite of all he'd

suffered himself, Will was strong and was trying to protect the others. Trying to save little Hank.

Julie gripped his hand as tension rippled through the air. "Tray, if you help us find Will and tell us where this man is holding the others, we can work out a deal for you."

"I won't go to jail?" Tray asked.

Brody released a pained breath as he waited on Julie's reply. This kid didn't belong in jail; he'd already spent years in prison.

"No, you won't go to jail," Julie said. "We'll see that you're reunited with your mother and receive the help you need to become a family with her again."

She meant counseling but she had deftly avoided the word. All the boys would need it, including Will.

But first they had to find the monster who'd kidnapped them.

"Do you have a mother, a woman who lives at the house?" Julie asked.

Tray shook his head. "Just Father."

"What is his name?" Brody asked.

Tray shrugged. "We just call him Father."

"But he has a job, doesn't he?" Julie asked. "You get bills? Have you ever seen his name on one of them?"

"No," Tray said. "He locks everything in his room. We aren't allowed in there."

"Where do you live?" Brody asked. "A house? Farm?"

"It's a compound," Tray said. "Like a camp only with barbed wire and cells."

"Cells?"

"Yeah, in the barn." He tugged at his bandage. "And there's a trailer where he goes sometimes."

"A trailer?" Julie asked.

Tray nodded. "He smells when he comes back."

Brody's stomach revolted. "Smells like what?"

"I don't know. Like smoke, some kind of chemicals maybe."

"He might be cooking meth," Julie guessed.

"How do we get there from here?" Brody asked.

"I…don't know," Tray said.

"But you left the place to go rob those stores," Julie said.

Tray twisted the sheet again, fear darkening his eyes. "Father doesn't let us go out on our own. He blindfolds us and drives us to the spot, then puts us out near the target store. When we're done, we meet him down the street."

Disgust filled Brody. So this monster threatened them, beat them, then blindfolded them so they couldn't lead anyone back to him if they were caught?

How in the hell were they going to find out where he kept the boys if Tray couldn't tell him? And what was happening to Will now?

If this monster thought Will had talked, would he kill him when he went back?

WILL FOUGHT THE instinct to run as Jeremy parked at the compound. Father had found a new place for them since he'd been caught.

This place had buildings made of concrete. The windows were boarded up.

There would be straps and chains inside just like the other place. Straps, chains and darkness.

An image of the BBL flashed through his head. There were beautiful pastures, stables, a creek, barns and a nice house. No barbed wire fences except to keep the cattle from wandering.

No boarded up windows. No chains in the bedroom. And a real kitchen where that nice Ms. Ellen cooked good-smelling pies and smiled at the kids when they came through the line to get food. They could get as much as they wanted, too. Then they told stories around a campfire and sang songs and went to bed on cots with real blankets and soft sheets.

But here there would only be the hard cold floor.

It was the way a soldier lived, Father told them.

And the pit—the pit made soldiers out of boys. Soldiers who knew how to survive if the enemy caught them.

His breath rattled in his chest. Brody didn't treat

the campers like soldiers though. He treated them like…he was their buddy.

Had Brody told him the truth? Would he help him if he escaped this compound? Would he help the others?

He had tried his best to remember how Jeremy had gotten here in case he had a chance to run.

But he couldn't leave without the others. He'd never live with himself if they got killed because of him.

Jeremy opened the truck door, and Will opened his own, every muscle in his body tensing as they entered the compound. He didn't see little Hank or Tray or the other two boys outside, but then Father rarely allowed them out.

He prayed they weren't all in the pit.

Jeremy nudged him through the gate, careful to lock it behind them, then Father stepped from the house.

His ice-cold eyes bore holes in Will, the leather strap he had slung over his shoulder slapping against his shoulder as he came to a stop in the dirt.

Brody's words traipsed through his head. *I love you, Will, I've never stopped looking for you. No one on my staff ever lays a hand to one of the campers.*

He hoped Brody hadn't lied. That he would keep looking for him.

But for now, Will had to be here, had to take whatever punishment Father doled out.

Unless Father decided to kill him.

Then Will would fight back. Because for the first time in years, he didn't want to die.

Chapter Fourteen

Julie fought panic. Will and the others were in danger. They had to hurry. With everything Tray had admitted, this unsub might just kill Will and the others, then disappear.

Then he'd resurface somewhere else, and he would continue his sick business, stealing other children from their families.

"Tray, what else can you tell me about where you live? Were there any neighbors around?"

He shook his head.

"What about any landmarks? Do you remember anything distinct? Is the compound near a river? Creek?"

"I don't know," Tray said, "We aren't allowed outside the fence."

"How about school?" Brody asked. "Did any of you attend school?"

"No, Father said the teachers brainwash kids. That they wouldn't understand our army."

"Army?" Brody asked.

Tray nodded. "He said God wanted men to have an army of men."

The unsub was obviously demented, maybe delusional.

"Tray, what kind of vehicle does your father drive when he takes you to rob the stores?" Julie asked.

Tray's eyes looked heavy, exhaustion evident on his face. "I know you're tired and you've been through a lot, Tray, but I need to ask you just a few more questions, then we'll leave you and let you rest. Okay?"

He nodded, pulling at the bandage as if it was bothering him.

"Was it a car, a truck? An SUV?"

"A van, black," Tray said. "The windows were tinted."

"What about the license plate?" Julie asked. "Do you remember the number? Was it a Texas tag?"

Tray's mouth twisted into a grimace. "I don't know," he said. "He changed it before we went out. I think he took tags off a junkyard."

Hope jolted through Julie. "Thank you, Tray, that might be helpful."

Tray yawned, and Julie patted his arm. "Hang in there, buddy, everything's going to be okay. You're safe now."

He gave her a tentative smile, then was asleep within seconds.

"Let's go, Brody. I want to get someone on that van right away."

"What about the junkyard?"

"That, too. If this bastard steals tags, he must not live far from a place where he can get them. We'll start looking for deserted areas near every junkyard in Texas."

And hope that they found Will and the others before their unsub panicked and disappeared—with or without those boys.

But at least there was one bright spot in the day—once they ran his DNA, they could contact Mrs. Goodner and tell her they had found her son.

BRODY FOLLOWED JULIE out to the waiting room where she phoned Chief Hurt and told him about the van. "Have Tech locate all the junkyards around San Antonio and Amarillo, then search for farmland, deserted houses or ranches, any place that is slightly off the grid where our unsub could hold his victims without anyone noticing what's going on." She hesitated. "Also, pull all the footage from the security cameras from the robberies. Look for a black van, tinted windows, nearby. Apparently the unsub drove the boys to the targeted stores and waited to pick them up. We might be able to get a shot of the unsub."

She shifted, digging some coins from her purse. "Yes. Really, that was fast." She rubbed her forehead. "All right, thanks."

When she hung up, Brody shoved his hands in his pockets. "What?"

"The boy in that bed is definitely Tray Goodner. Apparently he was fingerprinted when he was a child in one of those school programs to document kids, and the prints they took at the crime scene are a match."

"So you can let his mother know?"

"Chief Hurt already contacted her. She's on her way here now." Julie dropped the coins in the coffee machine and waited on it to fill the cup. "Finally a bright spot in this mess."

"WHAT'S GOING to happen to Tray?"

"I'll talk to the D.A., make him a deal."

Brody's mind raced. He would help the family if he could.

"I'm going to call my friend Johnny. He has a helicopter. Maybe he and Miles can scout out some areas for us."

Julie caught his arm. "Good, I'll have the analyst send whatever they find to Detective McGregor, but tell them if they see anything suspicious, to let us know. They are not to go in without backup."

"Got it." Brody stepped aside to phone Johnny

and Miles. He got them both on the line and gave them a rundown of the situation.

"You know I'll do whatever I can to help," Johnny said. "I'll gas up the chopper and be ready to go in half an hour."

"We'll find Will, Brody," Miles assured him. "Don't worry. He survived all these years because he's a tough kid like his brother."

Brody's throat thickened. These men might not be brothers, but they were close to it. And they lived by the cowboy code of honor.

He wanted to teach that code to Will, prove to him that not all men were monsters, that some were honorable. They respected their women and children and protected them instead of using and abusing them.

"Julie—Agent Whitehead—said her team will send you coordinates of where to search," Brody said.

"Hell, Brody, we know Texas. We'll start looking for junkyards and deserted farmland right away."

"I don't know how to thank you," Brody said.

Johnny cleared his throat. "No thanks necessary. You helped both of us when we needed it, and you gave us the privilege of working with the BBL."

Brody didn't know what to say to that. All the men who'd invested so far had made the place a success because they wanted to be there, not because of some duty or paycheck. They really cared about these troubled kids.

"Keep me posted. Oh, and guys, if you see anything suspicious, call me and Julie, and I will meet you there. She said to tell you not to go in on your own."

They agreed. The elevator doors slid open just as he ended the call, and a short woman with long brown hair, probably in her forties, raced in. She hurried to the nurse's station, wiping at tears on her cheeks. "My son... I received a call from the TBI, my son is here."

Julie was on the phone, so he nudged her. "That must be Tray's mother."

She nodded, ended the call, then the two of them met the woman at the nurse's desk.

"Mrs. Goodner?" Julie asked.

The woman's dark skin indicated she was part Hispanic. Apprehension warred with relief in her eyes. "Yes, my son, Tray, he's been missing five years. You found him?"

Julie nodded. "Yes, ma'am. We did."

Mrs. Goodner practically collapsed against Julie on a sob. "I can't believe it. I gave up." Her eyes turned toward Julie. "But he is alive?"

Julie coaxed the woman into a chair in the waiting room and Brody joined them.

"Where is he?" She gripped Julie's arms. "I have to see him. I have to give him a hug…"

"I know you're anxious," Julie said. "And I'll take you to him in just a moment. But we need to talk first."

Terror replaced the relief, and Mrs. Goodner began to tremble. "What? Where has he been? Is he hurt?"

Julie soothed her with soft whispered words, then explained how they had found Tray and what they believed had happened to him. "He has been abused," Julie said, her own voice cracking at the look of pain on Mrs. Goodner's face, "but he's strong and he's helping us try to find out where his abductor is holding the other boys."

"Others?" Mrs. Goodner cried. "How many others?"

"So far we think there have been ten over a twenty-year period, but we can't be sure until we catch him," Julie said.

"My little brother is one of them," Brody said, earning a compassionate look from the woman. "His name is Will. He and Tray were seen stealing from the convenience store together. And I think that the two of them protected the younger kids."

"Your son is very brave," Julie said. "But he will need therapy, Mrs. Goodner."

Her face looked tortured. "I…don't have insurance for that, but somehow I'll find a way."

Brody patted her hand. "Mrs. Goodner, I run a ranch called the BBL. It's a home with camps for troubled boys. I have counselors on-site there, and we have activities like horseback riding and calf roping that boys can do. It would be my honor if you and your son would stay there when he's released from the hospital. You can live in one of the cabins and Tray can receive counseling."

"But how do I pay you?"

"I have a scholarship fund," Brody said. "And since your son and my brother were friends, I think he's earned one."

Tears welled in Mrs. Goodner's eyes again, and Julie squeezed her shoulder. "Come on, let's go see your son."

"What do I say to him?" Mrs. Goodner asked, suddenly nervous.

"Just speak from your heart," Julie said.

Brody helped the trembling woman to stand, and the three of them walked to Tray's room. Julie knocked on the door, then they went in. Mrs. Goodner hesitated, then wiped at her eyes. "Tray?"

The boy rolled from his side to look at her, then his face crumpled. "Mama?"

Mrs. Goodner released a sob, then raced to his bed and dragged the boy in her arms. "Tray, I love you. I missed you so much, I thought I'd never see you again."

Brody blinked back his own emotions. At least Tray recognized his mother. That was a start, but he had a long road back.

And he would have mental scars just like Will.

God, he wanted Will back so they could get started on the process.

JULIE REMINDED HERSELF that reuniting Tray with his mother made her job worthwhile. But there were so many other boys missing.

And Will was back in the clutches of this monster and this young man Jeremy.

She'd heard of cases where abuseds repeated the cycle by becoming abusers, but she hadn't worked one to this degree before. The fact that Jeremy was helping his abductor ate at her.

Brody left Mrs. Goodner with his number and said he'd make the arrangements for her and Tray to stay at the BBL as long as they wanted and needed.

Julie couldn't help but admire his compassion and desire to help others.

They left the hospital and went to pick up some barbeque, but questions lingered, nagging at them both.

"I keep wondering what's happening to Will right now," Brody said. "And that little boy Hank."

Julie reached across the table and squeezed his hand. His gaze locked with hers, the silence filled with the worry plaguing both of them. But heat radiated from his fingers, and need flared in his eyes, reminding her of their earlier kiss.

And taunting her to ask for another.

To purge their tension by comforting one another.

But her cell phone jangled, and she checked the number. Seeing it was Chief Hurt, she quickly connected the call. "Agent Whitehead."

"We have three possible suspects who were ex-military and who lost sons. Alan Mitland, ex-Navy. His son died at birth while he was deployed. Then Cox Fuller. He lost his little boy in a custody battle because of alcohol addiction.

"And a man named Barry Moody. He also served in the marines, and when he returned, his wife had left with his son."

"We should divide up," Julie suggested.

"I agree. Cord will take Mitland and I'll track down Fuller."

"That leaves me with Moody. Where does he live?"

"His last known address was outside San Antonio, not too far from that ranch Brody owns."

Julie's pulse jumped. Maybe they finally had a lead. "Give it to me and I'll check it out."

He recited the address and Julie jotted it down on a napkin, then ended the call. Brody was already paying the bill.

"What?" he asked.

"Nothing concrete," she said, not wanting to give false hopes. "We were looking back at the original kidnapping, at what might have triggered it and ran a search on men who served in the military who had lost a child around that time period."

"You have a name?" Brody asked as they hurried to his Jeep.

"Yes," Julie said. "But it may not lead to anything, Brody. The odds that he would still be at that location are next to nothing. If he's come close to getting caught before, he would have moved around."

He cranked the engine. "And since some of the other kidnappings took place in different areas and these robberies were near Amarillo, he might be living somewhere closer to the area."

Julie nodded as he pulled from the parking lot. "I'm afraid with the news coverage about Hank and with Will getting caught, he may have already pulled up stakes again."

She gave Brody the address and he entered it into his GPS, then they fell into a pained silence as he drove.

Thirty minutes later, they veered onto a deserted country road that looked as if it hadn't been driven on in years. Dry scrub brush, mesquites and cacti filled the landscape, the sky a dismal gray. Occasionally a deserted farmhouse popped up, but if anyone lived out there they had to be a hermit.

Although it would make a perfect place for a compound.

Brody slowed as the wind tossed tumbleweeds across the barren land, then he spotted a rotting old farmhouse set off from the road. Barbed wire fencing surrounded the property, but even it looked ancient and was rusting and torn in places.

Brody wound down the dirt road, the tires spitting dirt and gravel, then slowed and they both scanned the property. "It looks deserted," Julie said.

Brody sighed. "Yeah, but let's check it out."

He parked and together they climbed out and walked up to the dilapidated house. The windows had been boarded up, there were holes in the porch floor and half the windowpanes were broken out.

He climbed through one, and knew immediately that the house was vacant. "There are raccoons and rats in here," he told Julie. "No sign that anyone's been here in a long time."

Julie shined a flashlight inside and grimaced in disgust. She'd been hoping at least to find signs that might lead them to this Moody man. But it didn't look as if there was any furniture or anything else inside.

"Stay out there, I'll check it out," Brody said.

Julie nodded, then shined the flashlight to make

a path and checked behind the house for outbuildings. But the only one she found looked as if it had been burned down.

She hurried back to Brody and met him just as he was climbing from the window. He had a piece of clothing that was rotting and filthy and was small enough to have been a child's. "I found this."

"I'll take it back and have forensics analyze it," Julie said. "If this man Moody is our guy, we might be able to match it to a victim."

Brody's phone buzzed, and he grabbed it from his belt then connected the call.

A second later, he gestured for her to get back in the car. "Okay, thanks, Miles. We're on our way."

"What?" Julie asked as she fastened her seat belt.

"They spotted a section of land that looked like it might be what we're looking for. No sign of anyone there, but there's a trailer and some outbuildings and barbed wire fencing surrounding it."

Julie prayed it wasn't a dead end as he sped away from the farmhouse.

PERSPIRATION BEADED BRODY'S neck as he raced toward the address. He hoped to hell this was the place they were looking for.

He wanted to find the bastard who'd hurt Will and the other boys and tear him apart limb by limb.

Julie remained silent, her anxiety evident in the

way she kept drumming her fingers up and down on the seat. The Jeep ate the miles, bouncing over ruts and ridges in the country roads. Storm clouds rolled in, threatening snow, the trees shivering in the wind.

An hour later, he veered down another desolate road, his stomach churning as they neared the place.

His phone buzzed and he snatched it up. It was Miles.

"We're going to land about a mile from the place just in case there's someone on the property. We don't want to alert them we're coming."

"Good idea," Brody said. "We're almost there."

He hung up and filled Julie in. She checked her weapon, and Brody winced. He had a rifle in the back, but he'd never used it on anyone.

"Have you ever had to shoot anyone?" he asked.

Julie's eyes darkened. "Once. A man charged me at an arrest."

"What did he do?"

"He killed four college girls," she said quietly.

Brody wanted to say more, but he spotted a locked gate up ahead and gestured toward it. "There it is."

Julie squeezed his arm. "Stay behind me, Brody."

He threw the Jeep to the right and parked between a group of trees. "The hell I will," he said as he reached over the back of his seat for his rifle.

"Brody," Julie said, tugging at his sleeve.

His jaw snapped tight. "We'll go in together," he said. "This is my brother we've come for. I'll take the damn lead."

Julie opened her mouth to argue, but he climbed from the vehicle, then retrieved bolt cutters from the back of his Jeep. Determined to protect Julie, he strode to the gate and cut the lock. He scanned the perimeter, noting a trailer in the distance along with two outbuildings.

Moving stealthily, he crept next to the trees, weaving between them as they approached.

"I don't see any vehicles," Julie said. "No black van."

Disappointment surged through Brody, but still they had to check it out. They inched closer and closer until the mobile home was within arm's reach.

"Look," Julie said, pointing behind the trailer to boxes of quart jars, distilled water and coffee filters.

But Brody had already reached for the door to the mobile home. As soon as he opened it, the pungent scent of ethyl ether assaulted him.

"It's a homemade meth lab," Julie said.

Then a strange sound filled the air, and Brody grabbed Julie's hand. "Come on, it's going to explode."

They ran toward the woods, but the explosion

rent the air, the force of it throwing them both to the ground a few feet away.

He tasted dirt, then he saw Julie lying on the ground, facedown. Panic slammed into him at the sight of blood trickling from her forehead.

Chapter Fifteen

Brody crawled over to Julie and eased her over.

"Julie?" He gently brushed her cheek, then removed a handkerchief from his pocket and wiped at the blood. Thankfully the cut was just a scratch.

Still, she could have been seriously injured.

"Julie, honey, are you okay?" Good God, he couldn't lose her. Not now.

Not again.

She slowly opened her eyes, confusion clouding them. "What happened?"

"The trailer blew."

"Not uncommon for homemade labs," Julie said, then pushed herself up to a sitting position.

Brody wanted to drag her back in his arms, hold her tight. Kiss her and tell her he would never let her go again.

But he didn't have that right.

"Brody, man, are you two okay?" Johnny yelled.

Brody straightened and stood as his friend approached. "Yeah, the damn trailer blew."

"We heard it," Miles said as he jogged toward them.

He helped Julie stand, and she brushed dirt and twigs off her slacks.

"Did you see anyone?" Johnny asked.

Brody shook his head no. "Did you?"

"No movement from the chopper, no sign of a car or van leaving, either. But we should search those outbuildings."

Smoke swirled above the trailer, the sickening odor of the ether wafting through the air. Brody gestured toward the wooden structures. "You two take that building, and Julie and I'll search the one to the left."

Miles led Johnny toward the right, and he and Julie headed to the left. The building looked like a garage or storage container, except as he entered, he noticed stalls on both sides.

"An old barn?" he said as he pulled open the wooden door.

Julie stepped inside, shining her flashlight across the space. "Perhaps the original owner put up the trailer as a temporary home until he could build a house."

"Or he planned the meth lab and needed buildings to house his supplies and product until he could move it," Brody suggested.

Inside the building was dark, the floor made of

dirt and straw. The stench of urine and sour sweat clogged the air, nearly making him gag.

"There's no one here," Brody said, disappointment mounting inside. Dammit, where was Will?

Julie walked to the first stall and shined the flashlight inside. "Oh, my God."

"What is it?" Brody moved up behind her, his stomach pitching as he realized what had upset her. Leather straps were attached to the posts of the stall, chains also wound around the posts.

Straps and chains that looked as if they had been used to tie an animal—or a child—inside the stall. They walked to each of the stalls and looked inside and found the same sick setup.

"I can't believe this," Julie said, her face paling in the dim light streaking through the barn. "He is a monster."

Brody opened the stall door and walked inside, raking his foot through the straw. He didn't know what he was looking for, maybe signs an animal had been kept there, not a person. He didn't find anything in the first stall, and Julie was searching the second, so he moved onto the third. The stream of light from the outside reflected off the stall door, and he knelt to examine it. The wood had splintered, with either a rock or fingernail marks embedded in the rotting frame as if someone had tried to claw their way out.

He examined the chains and leather strap marks next. His stomach revolted when he spotted bite marks in the leather.

"Someone was chained in here," he said. "There are teeth marks on the straps."

"Same in here," Julie said. "I'm going to get a forensic team out here. Our unsub may not be here now, but he was here. Maybe the lab can lift some prints we can use when we catch him."

When they caught him? Brody was beginning to wonder if they ever would.

Julie stepped outside the barn to make the call, and Brody followed, desperately needing some fresh air. Anything to erase the stench of what he'd just seen.

He spotted Miles and Johnny exiting the other barn and strode toward them. Miles disappeared around the outside of the barn, but Johnny was leaning against the door, his head down. The roar of the trailer fire echoed in the air, although the flames were starting to die down.

"Anything in there?" Brody asked Johnny.

Johnny's look of disgust mirrored his own feelings. "Straps and chains—"

"Same in there," Brody said, hitching his shoulder toward the other building.

"I can't believe a human could do that to another one," Johnny muttered.

Neither could Brody. Bile rose to his throat. But

he had a bad feeling the monster who'd kidnapped Will had chained him up like an animal. "Julie is calling a forensic team to process the buildings."

Miles suddenly appeared at the edge of the barn, his expression set in stone.

"What is it?" Brody asked.

"Not good."

Julie ended the call and joined them. "A forensics team is on the way." Her eyes narrowed as she realized something was wrong. "Did you find something else?"

Miles gave a clipped nod. "Two graves."

Brody staggered backward. Graves?

Dear God…had Moody killed Will when he'd returned and buried him out here where he thought no one would find him?

JULIE SHUDDERED, then noticed Brody's pallor turning gray and pulled herself together. Her phone buzzed, so she snapped it up.

"Mitland checked out," Chief Hurt said. "He lives with his mother and she verified that he's clean. Cord called and Fuller checked out, as well. He's remarried and they have a baby."

"Moody's the guy, Julie said. "We found a meth lab and the buildings where he kept the boys locked. There are also two graves."

"Good God," Chief Hurt said.

"I need a forensic team but let me check this out. I'll call you later."

Julie hung up, perspiration beading on her neck at the prospect of what they might find. Brody looked shaken as she gestured toward Miles. "Show me where they are."

Miles jerked his head, indicating for her to follow, and Brody snapped out of his shock. The three of them trailed Miles as he led them around the barn to the edge of the woods backing up to the building. Julie spotted the mounds of dirt and pushed her hair behind her ear.

The February breeze picked up, swirling the chemical odor and smoke from the fire around her. Julie knelt to examine the graves, looking for signs they were recent or any evidence the person who'd dug the graves had left behind. A loose button that had fallen off, a piece of fabric or human hair, anything that might help lead them to the unsub.

Brody suddenly disappeared, then returned a moment later carrying a shovel he must have found in one of the barns. "I have to see if Will is in there."

He jammed the edge of the shovel into the nearest grave, but Julie stood and grabbed the handle. "Stop it, Brody, you can't disturb the graves."

Brody wiped sweat from his forehead with his

sleeve. "I have to know," he murmured. "Move out of the way, Julie."

Julie's gaze met his. The torment in his eyes nearly sent her to her knees. But she couldn't allow him to destroy evidence. "I'm sorry, Brody, but I can't let you disturb the crime scene."

"I don't give a damn about your procedure," Brody shouted. "My brother might be in there."

Miles put his hand on the shovel. "She's right, Brody."

Brody glared at his friend. "But I have to know—"

"I understand you're terrified Will is in there, and we will have the graves dug up," Julie said softly. "But we have to wait on a team."

Brody's face twisted with emotions and Julie couldn't resist. She pulled him into her arms. "Listen to me, Brody, it's going to be all right."

"Not if Will is dead," Brody said in a raw whisper.

Miles took the shovel, and he knelt to examine the graves while Johnny walked around them.

"The grave looks as if it's been there for a while," Johnny said. "See how packed the dirt is."

Julie stroked Brody's back, but his shoulders shook. "There was blood in one of the stalls," he murmured.

Julie cupped his face between her hands and forced him to look at her. "We don't know that it's

Will's blood, Brody. Hang in there a little while longer."

He nodded against her, his breathing shaky, and Julie led him away from the site. She didn't stop until they'd reached where they'd parked. Instead of getting inside though, she pulled him down to a log on the ground beneath a cluster of trees where it was cool and the barns weren't visible.

She quickly phoned Chief Hurt and relayed the events, then asked him to send a coroner and ambulance so they could transport the bodies they were about to dig up. Brody remained silent, his body rigid with anxiety, his breathing labored in the quiet.

Night had set in, the moon a crescent sliver that fought its way through the storm clouds. Julie pressed a hand to Brody's back as he raised his knees, propped his elbows on them and rubbed his forehead. She hoped to hell the forensics team could finish before the snow came.

"I'm sorry I yelled at you," Brody said in a low voice.

"Don't worry about it," Julie said. "Just try to hold on to hope, Brody. Like I told you before, Will survived seven years. Now he knows you've been looking for him, he won't give up."

"But he didn't believe me," Brody said.

Julie sighed, wiping at dirt on her forehead. "He

may have said that, but on some subconscious level, the truth may have sunk in."

She twined her fingers with his, and they sat clinging to one another until the crime unit arrived.

Johnny and Miles met them at the CSU van, and Julie explained about the case and what they'd discovered. "Let's start with the graves," she said. "We need to identify them ASAP."

The team introduced themselves as Todd Franks, Janice Crimson and Detective Lyle Burks. A fire crew arrived next to extinguish what was left of the burning trailer and investigate the fire. Dr. Kurt Norman, the local coroner and medical examiner, drove up and Miles guided him to the scene.

Brody started to follow, but Julie shook her head. "Stay here, Brody. You don't have to watch this."

Brody gave her a sharp look. "I have to see for myself, Julie."

Their gazes locked for a long heartbeat but he didn't budge. Resigned, she nodded. "Come on, we'll watch together."

Johnny stood in the background while Todd and Janice photographed the scene and collected soil samples from the grave. Then Detective Burks and Todd began to dig.

Miles led Janice to one of the barns, and they began the laborious processing of the scene.

The sound of the shovel hitting dirt and rocks sounded ominous in the quiet as the men worked. The coroner stayed close, helping to rake away dirt when they reached the body.

Julie held one hand on Brody's arm to keep him calm as they unveiled the two bodies. The sight of the bones made Julie sick because those bones were human, and judging from the size they belonged to an adolescent.

But the bones had been there too long to be Will.

Brody must have realized it at the same time because his breath whooshed out. Then he turned and strode back toward the Jeep. She followed him and saw him leaning against the driver's door, his face ashen, sweat trickling down his neck.

"It's not Will," Julie said as she laid a hand on his shoulder.

Brody gave a short nod. "Thank God." Then he turned to her with a tortured look. "I'm so relieved. But I feel guilty for that."

"I know," Julie said. "Even if it's not Will, there are two boys who shouldn't have died."

EVEN AS BRODY admitted his guilt, relief swept through him. Sorrow for those kids in the grave and for their families overwhelmed him.

But Will might still be alive....

"I'm going to talk to the forensic team for a minute, then we're going home."

Brody didn't argue. There was nothing else they could do here. Hopefully the crime unit would find evidence to help track down this bastard.

But at least they had a name now. Barry Moody.

Although since the man had forced new names on his victims, he'd probably changed his own name, too.

Johnny walked over to him while Julie went to talk to the team. "We're going back to the BBL now, but we'll start looking again tomorrow," Johnny said. "As soon as it's daylight."

Brody shook his hand. "Thanks, I appreciate it."

Johnny nodded and tilted his hat to one side. "We won't stop until we find him, Brody."

Brody gritted his teeth as Johnny went to join Miles, and they headed back to the chopper. Brody tried to pull himself together, but his emotions were still ping-ponging all over the place as he and Julie drove back to the BBL.

As soon as they arrived and entered the house, he went straight to the bar in his office and poured himself a drink. Then he offered Julie one.

"I'm on duty," she said, although exhaustion laced her voice.

"You deserve it after today." Brody said.

Julie accepted the scotch and swirled it in her glass.

He sipped his drink. "Johnny and Miles are going to start again early in the morning."

"They're good friends," Julie said. "They care about you a lot, Brody."

"They care about kids," Brody said. "We...all have our stories."

"Yes, we do," Julie said softly, then she sipped her drink, a silent understanding passing between them.

Finally Brody knocked back his drink then set his glass on the table. "You were amazing today, Julie." He walked toward her, then brushed a strand of hair away from her cheek. "I...don't know how I would have made it through that without you."

Sadness glittered in Julie's eyes, then a flicker of some other emotion Brody couldn't define.

"You're strong, Brody," Julie said softly. "You always have been."

"No," he said, a knot in his belly. "I messed up years ago when I blamed you. I...needed you then but I pushed you away."

Julie lifted her hand and placed it over his. The touch sent a tingle of awareness and hunger through him. It had been a long damn time since he'd been with a woman.

Even longer since he'd made love to one, because the only woman he'd ever loved was standing in front of him.

"But I'm not going to push you away this time," he said gruffly. "I need you, Julie."

A heartbeat passed, then Julie set her glass on the table beside him and reached for him.

Chapter Sixteen

Julie threaded her fingers through Brody's hair, unable to resist the urge to comfort him.

Although as he drove his mouth over hers, kissing her with such fervor, desire flared inside her. She needed comfort as much as he did. Too many nights and days of monsters hurting women and children haunted her.

It had all started with Will years ago. It had to end with them finding him, bringing him back home, and helping him accept the love Brody had for him.

Brody emitted a low growl of pleasure as she parted her lips in invitation, and he took the kiss to a frenzied pace, his hands roaming over her shoulders down to her hips where he pulled her against his hard rippled body.

Her breath caught, delicious sensations pummeling her as his tongue danced with hers. He trailed kisses down her neck, nibbling at the sensitive flesh behind her ear, while she raked her hands over his muscled chest. She wanted his clothes off. Her clothes off.

To lie naked and loving him forever.

Then his teeth nipped at the buttons on her blouse, and her nipples stiffened to peaks that ached for his mouth.

Her back suddenly brushed the stair rail, and she realized they were in the foyer, that anyone could walk in and see them.

She kissed his neck, her body humming with arousal. "Upstairs," she whispered.

He murmured agreement, then swung her up in his arms and carried her up the stairs. She had never been in his room, but it was exactly as she would have imagined it. Masculine colors and furniture, strong lines, with pictures of horses and wildlife on the wall.

So Brody. The ultimate cowboy.

He shoved the comforter down and dropped her on the bed, then cradled her face between his hands and gazed into her eyes. His were dark pools of turmoil, pain and hunger.

Need flared inside her, a need that had been there years ago, one that had never left her. The years fell away, and she felt like she was seventeen again, hungry for Brody's touch, and so in love she could barely breathe.

"I've missed you so much," Brody murmured.

"I missed you, too," she whispered.

Raw passion flared on his face as he unbuttoned her blouse, then he lowered his head and claimed her mouth again. This time emotions drove the kiss, and his fingers trailed lower to rake over her breasts.

She arched into him, her pulse hammering as he kissed his way down her throat. Then he took one nipple in his mouth and suckled it while he unbuttoned her slacks, and she lifted her hips to allow him to undress her.

A frenzy of desire made her grip his hips and press herself against his hard erection. He groaned, then rose above her and stripped her underwear. Tiny shivers rippled through her as his fingers brushed her heat.

His look of approval made her reach for his shirt. The buttons flew to the floor as she ripped it off, then his jeans came next, the two of them becoming more frantic with each touch and passionate look.

She had always wanted Brody. He was the boy who had stolen her heart years ago.

And he was the man she wanted now.

BRODY SOAKED IN Julie's beauty, the sight of her naked body lying beneath his fueling his hunger. It had been so long since he'd held a woman, loved one, since he'd had Julie, that he wanted to prolong the pleasure.

She raked a hand through his hair, and he smiled, remembering the countless times she'd done that.

And how much he'd missed the intimate gesture.

Thoughts of that place they'd found earlier started to intercede, but he pushed the ugly truth away. He would hunt again tomorrow.

Pain and need blended together, making him reach for Julie and kiss her again. She plunged her tongue in his mouth, and he suckled it, using his hands to drive her to a frenzy as he toyed with her nipples, then slid a hand down to slide between her thighs. She parted her legs in silent invitation, moaning softly as he teased her folds then slipped two fingers inside her.

She whispered his name, clawing at his back, holding him tighter as he teased her again and again. White-hot need raged through him, the urge to thrust inside her almost unbearable.

Instead of satisfying himself, he raked his tongue down her breasts, then lower to her belly, then lower until he pushed her legs apart and settled his mouth where his fingers had been.

Julie murmured a low sound of pleasure, arching into him, and he tasted her sweetness, licking and suckling her sweet nub until she cried out his name and quivered with her orgasm.

But Brody didn't stop then. He continued pleasuring her with wicked tongue lashes and suckling noises while she trembled and sighed and begged him to enter her.

Finally Brody rose above her, then grabbed a condom from his jeans pocket, tore it open with his teeth and began to roll it on. Julie laughed as he struggled with it, then reached out to help him.

One touch of her fingertips, and he thought he would explode. Julie's eyes flickered with passion, igniting the heat in his body, and he kissed her again, then thrust inside her.

Julie gripped his arms and clung to him as he filled her, pulled out, then plunged into her again, over and over until she cried out his name in sweet oblivion. He lifted her hips and angled her so he could go deeper, until his body shook with erotic sensations so powerful that suddenly he came apart in her arms.

Pleasure so intense it made him growl her name stole through him, and he shuddered, rolling her to her side so he could cradle her in his arms. Their bodies were still joined, heat rippling between them, his heart racing from their lovemaking.

Julie curled into him, and he closed his eyes, holding her tightly, afraid if he released her, he'd lose her again.

JULIE DRIFTED TO sleep, sated and feeling more alive—and loved—than she had in years.

Hours later, she awakened, her cell phone trilling. For a moment, she considered not answering it. She didn't want to leave the sanctity of Brody's arms.

But Will was still missing, and so was little Hank Forte.

Brody moaned, and slowly opened his eyes, but a dark cloud passed over them when he realized the phone was ringing.

Julie sat up, tugged the sheet up to cover her breasts, then grabbed the phone. The caller ID showed the CSU number. "Special Agent White-head."

"Agent Whitehead, this is Detective Burks from the crime unit."

Julie scrubbed a hand through her hair. "Yes?"

"We're still sorting through the prints we found at the crime scene, but we've identified the two bodies in the graves. Carl Fanning and Daryl Derwin. They've been there a long time."

"What about Will Bloodworth's fingerprints? Did you find those?"

"Yes," he said. "But so far we haven't found Hank Forte's."

"So this man Moody must have moved before he kidnapped Hank."

"I can't say for sure, but with the meth lab explosion we're still working on the timing."

"Thanks."

"We're going to do autopsies, of course, and contact the families."

Brody climbed from the bed and went into the bathroom, and she heard the shower kick on. She wanted to join him, to continue their lovemaking, to feel happy and alive and forget about the world of ugliness surrounding her, but the phone call had definitely killed the intimacy.

Frustrated, she grabbed her clothes, hurried to the guest room across the hall and jumped in the shower herself. By the time she emerged dressed and ready to work, she found Brody in the kitchen with coffee and breakfast.

"I talked to Johnny and Miles, and they're going back out to search." He handed her a cup of coffee, and their hands brushed. His were big, dusted with hair, and had brought her intense pleasure the night before.

For a heartbeat of a second, hunger darkened his eyes, but his phone buzzed again and reality interceded as he answered the call.

"Yes." A pause. "Okay, I'll meet you and Tray at the main house counseling center in five minutes."

Julie's stomach growled and she sat down and ate the scrambled eggs and toast he'd made. Brody joined her a second later.

"Mrs. Goodner and Tray are on their way here."

"It's nice of you to offer them a place to stay."

Brody shrugged and wiped his mouth with his

napkin. "God, Julie, it's the least I can do. They've both been through hell."

He would know because he'd been there himself.

He polished off his breakfast, and she did the same then they worked in tandem to clean up the dishes. It felt so familiar that Julie felt as if they'd been doing it for years.

As if they belonged together.

But she couldn't get her hopes up for a future. Last night had been about comfort. And maybe a glimpse of the past.

But they still had to find Will, and if Brody lost him again…

No, she couldn't think like that.

Brody grabbed his Stetson and she tucked her phone onto her belt then they went to meet the Goodners.

Tray looked bruised, his skin still a grayish color, and his bandaged arm was in a sling. His eyes darted around nervously as Brody greeted him and his mother.

"Did you get any sleep last night?" Julie asked Mrs. Goodner.

"Not much," the woman admitted. She lowered her voice so her son couldn't hear. "I was so excited to have my boy back, but when I think of what he went through…" Tears blurred her eyes and Julie squeezed her shoulder.

"I know it's difficult, but today your son can start to recover." She gestured for her to sit at the round table in the corner. "We hope we find the other boys and they can have that chance, too."

BRODY SYMPATHIZED WITH Tray and his mother as they settled into his office. Kim, Brandon Woodstock's wife who counseled kids at the BBL, had agreed to sit in and was eager to help Tray.

Brody claimed the chair across from Tray and pushed a can of soda toward him. "I'm sorry for what happened to you," Brody said. "And this is not an interrogation, Tray. I swear, no one here is out to trick you or hurt you or pin something on you."

Kim spoke up. "He's right, Tray. We're not here to judge or condemn you and nothing you say can be used against you."

Tray jerked a thumb toward Julie. "What about her?"

Julie sipped her coffee, her smile warm, welcoming. "I am a TBI agent, Tray, but no matter what you've heard about the police or federal agents, I only want to help you and find the other missing boys."

Mrs. Goodner twisted her hands together on the table. "We do want to help you," she said. "But my son has been through so much."

Tray squared his shoulders, his shirt too big

for his thin frame. He looked nervous, but Brody could also see that he was trying hard to be a man.

"I'm okay, Mom." His gaze met Brody's. "I want to do this."

"You knew my brother, Will?" Brody asked.

Tray nodded. "Father called him Kyle."

"What did he call you?" Kim said softly.

"RJ." Tray ducked his head down. "But I never forgot my real name."

Every muscle in Brody's body tightened. Had Will really forgotten or was something else going on?

"We found a compound with barn stalls and a meth lab in a trailer," Julie said. "Is that where he kept you?"

Tray rubbed his finger around the soda can. "For awhile. We left there when you caught Kyle."

"But the meth lab was still being used," Julie said.

Tray shrugged. "I guess he went back and worked it some. Money was tight and the heat was on. That's why he started sending us out to rob the stores."

A moment of silence passed, the harshness of his admission lingering between them all.

Finally Kim broke the quiet. "Tray, where did you go from there?"

Tray's hand trembled as he picked up the soda can and took a sip. "Some place with concrete buildings." He closed his eyes, his pale face constricting as if he was remembering a horror from his past.

"What else was there?" Kim said in a low soothing voice. "A house? Was it a farm?"

Tray shook his head. "Some tunnels."

"What kind of tunnels?" Brody asked. "Like an underground mine?"

"Were there trucks there? Had someone been working them?" Julie asked.

Tray opened his eyes, fear flashing in the depths. "No, it… No one was there. It was away from everything, like it hadn't been used in a long time. There was rusted equipment left behind."

Brody snapped to attention, his mind racing. "An old abandoned oil mine." He patted Tray's shoulder. "That's good, Tray. Thank you."

Kim offered Tray a smile, and his mother put her arm around him and gave him a hug. "You are a brave boy, my son."

Tray beamed beneath the praise, giving Brody hope that he would eventually overcome the trauma of his ordeal.

"Do you remember anything else?" Julie asked.

Tray looked at his mother, pain wrenching his face. "Jeremy brought Hank there," he said, his voice cracking. "Will…he tried to protect the little guy. But when he got caught, Father was real mad."

Brody and Julie exchanged worried looks.

"What did he do?" Kim asked gently,

Tray closed his eyes again. "He said he might have to move again." In spite of his bravado, Tray dropped his head forward and held it between his hands.

"Why does moving upset you?" Kim asked.

Silence, thick and daunting, echoed in the room. Then Tray answered, his voice a low tortured sound. "Because he's scared to move us all."

Brody's blood ran cold. That was the reason there were two bodies at the meth lab site. Although they had been there a while.

Rage and disgust filled him, but then he remembered that in Tray's story, he'd given them a lead.

"I'm sorry for what happened to you, Tray, but thank you for your help." He shook the boy's hand then hugged his mother. "You two are welcome here as long as you want. The BBL will always be your home."

He grabbed his cell phone and punched Johnny's number as he left the room. "I have a lead," he said as soon as Johnny picked up.

"We're heading to the chopper now. Just tell us where to go."

Brody told him about the drilling site, and Johnny jumped on it. "We'll start searching right away."

"You know," Brody said. "I think I may know

a place to check out. Some property I looked at when I was thinking about setting up the BBL."

He gave Johnny the coordinates, then stepped back in the room to get Julie. They had to go now. Every second counted.

Will and Hank needed them.

He would die before he let his brother down this time.

Chapter Seventeen

Julie phoned Chief Hurt to inform them about the information Tray had given them.

"Brody knows an area where an abandoned mine is," Julie said.

"If you get there and find anything, call for backup," Hurt said. "You have to consider this unsub armed and dangerous."

"I will." She strapped on her holster, jammed her service revolver in it, then yanked on her jacket.

Brody watched her, his dark eyes hooded. "You shouldn't be doing this work, Julie. It's too dangerous."

Anger slithered through her. "Let's go."

He kept a rifle in the back of his Jeep, unloaded since he worked with the kids, but he had ammunition in the glove compartment. But he grabbed his .38 revolver and stuffed it in the waist of his jeans.

"Do you have a permit for that?" Julie asked.

Brody made a sarcastic sound. "Are you really

going to preach to me about the law when we're hunting down a violent, demented child killer?"

"I just don't want you to get hurt…or in trouble." She touched his shoulder, her fingers tingling from the contact. Just a few hours ago, they had lain sated and naked in each other's arms. Now, it was almost like that moment hadn't happened.

As if it hadn't meant anything special to Brody.

"Don't worry about me, Julie. I can take care of myself."

And he would kill and put his life on the line to save his brother, even if it meant going to jail. She saw that truth in his eyes.

He shouldn't be going with her. He was too close to the case.

But there was no use in telling him that because she knew he wouldn't listen.

At least if they were together maybe she could control the situation.

Brody didn't wait for her to comment. He grabbed his keys, opened the door and they headed to his Jeep. Tension made the air thick in the car, and Julie considered broaching the subject of the night before, but judging from the tight set of Brody's rugged jaw, sex was the last thing on his mind.

So she let the silence linger.

He sped up, crossing from the main road to a dirt road that looked desolate. Trees flew past, the scenery blurring. Winter had turned the grass brown, bushes looked desperate for water and more sun, but the gray clouds and the chill in the air made it look as if it might snow. Rare for this part of Texas, but occasionally a snowstorm blew through.

The wind whistled through the windows, sending dust swirling behind them. "I think Tray is going to be okay," she said, finally breaking the awkward silence.

Brody murmured something she couldn't understand. "Maybe."

"He will," she said, vying for optimism. "Of course he needs counseling, but he's strong and his mother loves him. Having someone who cares about you goes a long way in overcoming a trauma." Maybe she and Brody would both have been better off if they'd realized that years ago and supported each other instead of blaming themselves and one another.

"He may learn to cope, but he'll never forget what happened to him, what he saw."

"No, he won't," Julie said. "But people either let adversity destroy them or they let it make them stronger. Tray and Will both obviously did what they had to do to survive, but they also protected the younger kids. That takes guts, courage and the kind of strength that means they'll not only survive, but turn out to be leaders."

Brody worked his mouth from side to side. "I hope you're right."

They bypassed several rotten, deserted houses then she spotted barbed wire fencing and some concrete buildings in the distance.

She pointed them out, her pulse jumping. "Over there."

"I see it," Brody said as he whirled the Jeep down the long drive.

Half a dozen shade trees dotted the land, and a piece of equipment that looked like it had belonged to an oil driller had been abandoned and was rusting by one of the three concrete buildings. "Looks like there was once a digging crew here," Julie commented.

"Yeah, they didn't find oil," Brody said. "So it was abandoned and Moody moved in with his victims."

Julie shuddered as Brody parked. Time to go in and see if anyone was here now.

She just prayed they didn't find any more graves.

BRODY EASED THE JEEP beneath a pair of Mexican olive trees.

Julie wrestled her hair into a ponytail. "Are Miles and Johnny coming?"

"They were checking out a couple of different spots so we could cover more territory, then they were going to fly here."

Julie slid from the car, removed her gun and gripped it by her side. He did the same, the two of them creeping through the bushes and trees along the woods until they drew closer to the first building.

Brody removed a pair of wire clippers from his pocket, cut the fence apart enough for them to crawl through, then led the way through the hole. Weeds and the overgrown grass flattened beneath his boots as he stepped forward.

Julie arched her head to scan the area, then tugged at his elbow. "Over there, there's the black van we've been searching for."

Brody's pulse clamored. The man who'd held Will had driven a black van. "I should call for backup."

"Just text Miles that we think we found the place."

Julie did, then signaled to Brody to move ahead. They crouched low, ducking behind bushes in case the unsub was watching. Although everything around them seemed eerily quiet.

The wind that had been blowing had died down, the air steeped with the scent of dirt and clay and…his own fear.

He breathed it in and out as if it was a live beast choking him.

Sweat trickled down the back of his neck, then

the sound of a vulture flying above rent the air, and panic hit him.

God, please don't let us be too late.

He made it to building one, noting in disgust that all the windows had been boarded up. A quick glance at the other buildings indicated the same condition.

Julie brushed his arm. "I'm going in."

"Me first," he whispered.

She shook her head, but he pushed past her and examined the lock. Easier to pry the boards off the window than to break it. He scanned the property again, his senses honed, listening for sounds indicating someone was inside.

Again the eerie quiet engulfed him, making him think that Moody had already left this place. But how? Had he realized the police were searching for the black van and confiscated another ride?

He clenched his jaw then used his hands to rip off one of the boards. The wood was rotting and splintered in two easily, then he tore off another and another until he could see inside. He pulled a small flashlight from his pocket and shined it inside the building. "I don't see anyone," he said.

"Let me climb through the window and check it out," Julie said.

"No, I will." Brody caught her by the arm but she shook her head.

"Listen, Brody, I'm smaller and will fit easier. Just stand watch and keep your eyes peeled."

He gave a reluctant nod, and boosted her so she could crawl through the window. Her flashlight beam panned the inside, and he watched as light fell across the corners.

Julie hissed. "This is as bad as the other place."

More leather straps and chains.

Rage rolled through him. This bastard didn't need to go to jail; he deserved to die.

Julie returned and he helped haul her through the window, then they moved to the second building. Again, he pried the boards off the window and scanned the inside with his flashlight.

"We'll have to get forensics out here," Julie said.

Dammit. He didn't want evidence. He wanted to find the man and beat the living daylights out of him.

The sound of the vultures ahead rattled him again, intensifying his nerves as they crossed the field to the last building. He scanned left and right, searching for a drill site or a place where the mines might have been built if they'd gotten that far.

Tray had said there were tunnels. But he didn't see any. They must be close by though.

Julie walked over to examine the van while he tore the boards off the windows of the last structure. The moment he looked inside, he realized this place looked more like a house inside. The other two had small cubicles like stalls, but this one had a hallway and rooms on each side. He also spotted a kitchen.

Was this where Moody slept and lived while the boys were locked up like animals?

Julie slipped up behind him. "It has to be the van," she said. "There were ropes inside and a whip."

Brody's jaw ached from gritting his teeth. He hoisted Julie inside the house, and peered inside, trying to see as she waved her flashlight around inside.

"Do you see anything?" he asked.

"Magazines on weapons, some underground newspapers citing conspiracy theories." She cursed. "The man was building an army to protect himself."

Brody grimaced. That was the reason he chose boys, and the reason they weren't sexually abused. He'd tried to beat them into being soldiers.

"Oh, my God," Julie said.

"What?"

"Listen, I hear something."

Brody's heart skipped a beat. If someone was in there, he had to go inside. He had to protect Julie.

JULIE SCANNED THE living room, disgusted when she saw a wall display of pictures of all the boys

Moody had kidnapped. His Wall of Glory, he had labeled it, His Army.

Dear God, what acts of horror had the man who lived here committed?

A soft banging sound reverberated from down the hallway again, and she raced toward it.

She checked the room to the left. Judging from the size of the military boots on the floor, it was Moody's.

But the sound had come from the right. Behind her, she heard Brody kicking open the front door, then a whimpering sound, barely discernible, reached her ears.

She raced across the hall then halted at the door, listening, the sound so painful that she could hardly breathe.

Nerves on edge, she lowered her gun to her side, then hurried to the door and tried to open it. The house was old, the door locked with an old fashioned kind of key. She quickly spun around in search of it.

"What is it?" Brody asked as he stormed into the room.

"Someone's locked in the closet," she said on a raspy breath. "I think it's a little boy, probably Hank. I heard him crying."

Pain wrenched Brody's face, and he crossed the distance to the door and jerked on it. It didn't budge.

"Listen," Brody said gruffly. "We're here to help you so don't be afraid. I'm going to kick the door in. So scoot back as far as you can."

Another whimpering sound echoed back.

"It's okay," Julie said through the door. "I'm a law officer, we came to take you back to your mother."

Brody took a step back, then raised his foot and slammed his boot against the door. Inside, the boy cried out.

Once, twice, three times and Brody kicked it open. Julie's heart ached as she knelt and saw the little boy hunched in the back of the dark closet. Tears streaked his pale face, his T-shirt was torn, his lip trembling.

Still, even dirty and shrouded in the dark, she recognized him immediately.

It was Hank Forte.

"Hey, sweetie," Julie said softly. "It's all right, my name is Julie."

His big eyes were filled with terror. "I want my mommy."

Julie's heart broke. "I know you do, and I'm going to take you home to her, okay?"

He had drawn his knees up to his chest and had his arms wrapped around them so tightly his hands looked bone-white. There were also rope marks that made her shiver inside.

"Julie's right," Brody said, kneeling beside her.

"We're here to get the bad man who took you away from your mommy and daddy."

Julie held out her arms. "Come here, Hank. We won't ever let him hurt you again. I promise."

Hank's little face crumpled again, tears spilling over, and Julie reached for his hand, taking it gently in hers. A second later, he collapsed in her arms, sobbing and trembling.

Brody helped her stand, his gaze meeting hers. She could just imagine what he was thinking—that his little brother had hidden and cried like this and hoped someone would come for him but nobody had.

Julie patted and rubbed Hank's back, soothing him with hugs and kisses and whispered words of comfort.

Brody jerked his head toward the door. "Let's get him out of here."

The sound of the chopper rumbled in the distance and she knew help would soon arrive.

Brody cradled her and Hank against him, and they ran out of the house and back toward the Jeep. When they neared it, Julie opened the door and sank into the backseat with Hank. "It's going to be all right, sugar." She gently stroked his hair back from his face and examined him. He didn't have any visible bruises.

Maybe they'd saved him in time.

"Hank," Brody said, leaning in and squeezing

the little boy's shoulder. "We know you aren't the only boy he was holding. Where are the others?"

Terror seized Hank's face again, and he dug his fingers into Julie's arms with a death grip.

"We want to help those boys, too," Julie said. "And make sure this man goes to jail and never hurts anyone else again."

Hank studied them for a pain-filled minute, then nodded.

"Were they here?"

He nodded again.

Julie stroked his back again, soothing him. "Where are they now?"

"The p…it," Hank said.

Julie blinked, wrapping her arms tighter around the trembling boy. "What do you mean, the pit?"

"Where is this place?" Brody asked, his voice raw.

Hank released one hand from Julie's neck, then lifted it and pointed toward the woods in the distance.

"Are they there now?" Julie asked.

Hank nodded. "The mean old man said that we had to move but the others had to stay here."

Julie swallowed back revulsion. "Stay with him," she told Brody. "I have to go."

"No." Brody gently pushed her back into the seat with the boy. "I'm going. Hank needs you right now."

Then he turned and raced away from the Jeep just as Miles and Johnny landed in the field.

BRODY RAN toward the woods, his body tense with rage. He just prayed he was in time.

The wind that had died earlier picked up, swirling dead leaves around his feet, and making the trees shake. A few feet in, and he noticed footprints and forced himself to follow them instead of running blindly ahead.

Leaves rustled, the clouds growing darker by the second, a chill in the air that seemed more from his fear than the temperature.

He spotted broken twigs, flattened brush, then a piece of a plaid shirt caught on a tree.

The shirt Will had been wearing when he'd run away with Jeremy.

He struggled to breathe then listened for sounds and heard footsteps behind him. He'd heard the chopper land, so assumed it was either Julie, Johnny or Miles coming to back him up.

A tree branch slapped him in the face, but he trudged on, hoping it was Miles, not Julie. He didn't want her in danger anymore.

He wanted her home with him on the ranch.

Voices drifted in the breeze, and he slowed his pace, inching closer and moving stealthily, determined to sneak up on Moody. Was Jeremy with him now? The two of them working as a team?

How many boys did he plan to leave in that pit?

The voices echoed again, and he crept closer, peering through the bushes at the clearing. Old tools lay rusted and broken in a pile by a hole. This was the hole that led down to the tunnels Tray had talked about.

A tall, big guy with close-cropped hair, wearing army fatigues, paced back and forth by the hole, but he couldn't see his face. He carried an army assault rifle over his shoulder just as a good soldier would.

He had to be Moody.

A tall, lanky boy also dressed in fatigues stood beside him, weapon poised and pointed at the hole. Judging from the photo and sketch he'd seen, it was Jeremy.

He removed his own weapon and clicked off the safety. Needing to get closer, he inched past a few more trees then veered to the right to get a better view.

A cold knot of terror seized him at what he saw. Two boys were on their knees in front of the hole. Lewis Renz and Phil Jasper.

Will had planted himself in front of them, his look feral.

He was trying to protect the boys.

Dammit. He was going to get himself killed trying to save them.

Chapter Eighteen

Julie and Miles veered closer to Brody, fear clogging her throat at the sight of Brody facing down Moody.

Jeremy also had a gun and looked as if he would use it, as if he'd do anything to protect this man the boys called Father.

Johnny had stayed back with Hank to wait on an ambulance and for Hurt and Cord. Knowing the little boy was safe was a small victory when two more boys were huddled together at the edge of the pit.

Will was on his knees as if he was expecting an execution.

Had Moody planned to kill him, then leave the others inside the pit to die?

Then Will looked up and must have seen Brody, because his eyes flickered with hope. Brody eased through a patch of weeds, moving closer to Moody so he could sneak up behind him.

"You have been warned, Kyle," Moody said.

"You are a traitor. You have defied your father and our team. Now it is time for your punishment."

The other boys looked terrified, but Will jutted up his chin.

Julie motioned for Miles to go right while she went left. Maybe Brody could distract Moody long enough for them to save the other kids.

But before they could reach the woods behind the boys, Brody moved in on Moody. He slipped up behind him and thrust his gun at the back of Moody's head.

"Drop it, Moody, or you're dead."

The world spun into chaos then. Instead of complying, Moody whirled around and jabbed the butt of his rifle into Brody's stomach.

Julie froze, fear paralyzing her. Dear God, no. She couldn't lose Brody now.

BRODY STARED INTO the cold sinister eyes of the man who had stolen his brother, and couldn't believe what he saw. Moody almost looked like a normal man.

Just someone you would pass on the street without noticing.

Yet a sickness plagued him that, once he looked closer, brimmed in the man's crazed expression.

"Tell Jeremy to drop the gun," Brody said firmly. Moody's sarcastic laugh rent the air, fueling Brody's temper. "Tell him, Moody. It's over."

Moody jammed the gun harder into Brody's belly, and Jeremy pointed his weapon at Will. But instead of giving in, suddenly Will jumped Jeremy.

Brody's heart hammered, but the movement shocked Moody into looking around, and Brody lunged toward him. He knocked Moody's rifle from his hand with one hard swipe. Jeremy's gun went off, a shot ringing through the air, and Brody prayed his brother hadn't been hit.

"Will?" he shouted.

"I'm okay," Will yelled.

But neither of them were okay. Moody lashed out at Brody with his fists, knocking him to the ground. They rolled in the dirt, exchanging blow for blow.

Sweat and blood trickled down his forehead, and he tasted dirt, but he was determined to win. Moody grunted as Brody punched him in the belly, then pummeled his face.

Grunts and groans from Will and Jeremy echoed around him as they fought. Julie and Miles rushed to the boys by the pit and ushered them to the edge of the woods to safety.

Jeremy had lost his rifle, but crawled toward it, and Will saw he was going for the gun and went after him.

Meanwhile, Moody went for Brody's pistol, which had flown against a rock. Brody grabbed

Moody's ankles and dragged him through the dirt, then climbed on his back. He tried to choke him, but Moody somehow found a rock and twisted enough to hit him in the side of the head with it. For a moment, Brody's head spun. Just enough time for Moody to roll from under him and reach the rifle.

Will and Jeremy rolled in the dirt, then Will lunged up and went back for the gun. But Jeremy flew at him and knocked him against a rock. Will's head hit the edge, and he staggered back and collapsed on the ground, his head bleeding.

Miles suddenly attacked Jeremy, putting the kid into a chokehold. "It's over, son."

"Put the gun down, Moody," Julie shouted.

Brody wiped at the blood and sweat in his eyes, then Moody swung the rifle toward Julie.

His heart nearly stopped.

He couldn't let the bastard kill the woman he loved.

All the rage and anguish he'd held inside for years surged through him, and he vaulted forward and caught Moody by the knees, taking him down. The gun fired into the air, and Moody tried to turn it on Brody, but Brody clawed at it.

"Give it up, Moody!" Julie yelled.

But Moody was mean as hell and had trained to fight.

He gripped the rifle, his finger nearing the trigger. Brody saw Will's face in his mind and knew he had to stop Moody or he would hurt someone else's child or brother.

He gritted his teeth, then snatched the gun. They fought for it again, but this time Brody pushed Moody onto his back, then wrapped one hand around Moody's neck, squeezing him so hard that Moody's eyes bulged.

He continued the pressure while Moody wheezed for air, but Moody was weakening and his fingers slowly slipped from the gun. Brody tossed it away, then climbed on Moody, straddling him as he wrapped his other hand around the man's neck.

Moody cursed, but his words sounded faint as Brody squeezed harder. Brody had never hated anyone like he hated this man. Moody had taken half a lifetime from him, from Julie, from his brother.

He deserved to die.

Brody's fingers closed tighter, a smile creasing his face as the man's face grew ashen, his mouth hanging open in vain as he gasped for air.

A shot rang in the air, and he jerked his head sideways to see what had happened.

Julie stood with the gun in the air. "That's enough, Brody, let him go."

Miles held Jeremy in handcuffs and he spotted Will rousing from unconsciousness.

"Brody, please," Julie said as she met his gaze.

"Will's seen enough violence. Let us take Moody to jail where he belongs. The families of the other victims deserve for him to have to face them."

Brody glanced back down at Moody. His eyes had rolled back in his head, but he was still hanging on.

Julie was right. Will had seen enough violence. And he didn't want to end up in jail when Will was free now and needed him.

He dug his knee into the man's groin though before he released him and stood. Julie strode over and rolled Moody over, then slapped handcuffs on him while Brody raced over to Will.

Sirens wailed in the distance, indicating help was on the way.

Will moaned, and reached for his head, touching the blood, and Brody pulled him up against him and held him until the paramedics arrived.

By the time they carried Will to the ambulance, Chief Hurt and Agent Cord had arrived to take Moody into custody. Brody and Julie and Miles herded the other boys toward the ambulance to join Hank.

Brody ached for them as the medics helped them into the ambulance. He would offer their families help just as he had Tray's.

Then he moved up beside Will where he lay on the stretcher, a bandage wrapped around his head.

"You were a hero today, Kyle," he said.

Tears blurred his brother's eyes, and he shook his head. "My name is Will. I remember you, Brody."

Emotions swelled in Brody's throat, tears flooding his eyes as his brother reached for him.

Brody wrapped him in his arms, for the first time in seven years, smiling through the pain because now he believed that Will would somehow be all right.

Julie's heart squeezed as she watched Brody reunite with his brother. Seven long years and he'd never given up.

Her heart was still pounding with fear from watching him nearly choke Moody though. She understood his fury, but the last thing she'd wanted to do after finally ending this nightmare was to have to arrest Brody.

But it still wasn't over.

There were three boys that needed to be reunited with their family members. Hank, Lewis and Phil.

They also had to question Moody about Anthony Putnam and Jeff Wickman. Her gut told her they were dead, but she had to know. Their families deserved closure.

Chief Hurt approached her. "I'll drive Moody back to headquarters and process him."

Julie glanced at Jeremy. "I don't know what

to do with him. He needs serious therapy but we can't discount his part in kidnapping Hank."

"Sad," Chief Hurt murmured. "We can probably get him in a psychiatric hospital for treatment."

Julie nodded. "Let me talk to Brody for a minute. Then I'll meet you at the TBI."

Chief Hurt dragged a half unconscious Moody toward his car and pushed him into the backseat. Agent Cord took Jeremy from Miles and did the same.

"You can't take me away from my father," Jeremy snarled.

Julie simply gave him a pitying look. None of this was his fault, but she was afraid he was too traumatized to recover.

Brody looked up at her from the ambulance where he was sitting beside Will. They both looked haggard but a smile worked its way through.

Brody stepped from the ambulance, his smile fading. "Dammit, Julie, you almost got yourself killed."

Julie had expected a thank-you, not a reprimand. "So did you, Brody. But we saved Will, and that's all that matters."

Anger suffused her. "Johnny can take you to the hospital, I'm going to the TBI to question Moody."

Brody grabbed her arms, his expression feral. "Walk away from it, Julie. You don't belong there with those monsters."

Julie lifted her chin. "Where do I belong, Brody?"

Brody's gaze latched with hers, a myriad of emotions flickering in the depths, but the ambulance driver announced they were ready to roll, and Johnny appeared, and Brody didn't reply.

Disappointment filled Julie. She'd wanted him to tell her she belonged with him.

But too much had happened between them. And now he had Will back, he had to focus on helping his brother recover.

THE NEXT WEEK Brody and Will spent talking and making up for lost time. Will had shared some of what had happened to him, and as painful as it was to hear, Kim assured Brody that it meant Will was making progress.

Will still had nightmares, but he admitted that he fought them because he knew now that he had a home and a brother who loved him.

He was a natural with the animals and also had warmed up to some of the boys and was making friends. He and Carlos seemed to have bonded. He'd also found some kindred spirits on the BBL.

Ms. Ellen had made it her project to fatten him up. Will already treated the sweet, kindhearted cook like family, like the grandmother he'd never had.

Brody smiled, watched him working with Carlos to groom two of the quarter horses they'd taken for a ride. He had everything he'd wanted for so long. His ranch, the BBL, his little brother back.

He had everything except for Julie.

Her short phone call after Johnny had whisked him to the hospital to be with Will after the arrests still disturbed him. She had sounded the same… yet distant. As if now the case was over, she was moving on.

He didn't want her to move on. Not without him anyway.

But she'd gone back to the TBI to question Moody. How could he stand to live with her if she continued to do that job? He'd constantly be terrified she wouldn't come home at night.

Hell, she could have gotten killed a dozen times these past few years.

And he would never have known because he had let her go.

Dammit. He tied his own horse to the rail.

He couldn't let her go now, could he?

Will finished with his horse, then strode toward him, a smile fighting with the wary look that dogged him when the dark memories crept back to taunt him.

"There's supposed to be a special news report about the case," Will said.

Brody grimaced. All of the staff and most of the counselors were aware of what Will had endured, at least that he'd been kidnapped and held for years.

Brody slung his arm around his brother's shoulder. Already Will was putting on muscle, his skin glowing from the fresh air. "Do you really want to watch it?"

"No," Will said. "But we both have to face it. I can't run or live in the dark anymore."

Emotions welled in Brody's throat. He was so damned proud of his brother he wanted to cry.

But he and Will had shed enough tears and heartache, so he clapped him on the shoulder and together they walked back to the house. They washed up, then met in the den to watch the newsfeed.

Chief Hurt and Julie appeared in the pressroom, both looking worn and tired. Still, Brody's breath caught at the sight of her, his heart beating double-time.

The reporter introduced herself, then gestured for them to take the podium. The room was filled with reporters, all anxious to hear the story on Moody and his twenty-year reign of terror.

"It is true that we have arrested a man named Barry Moody for the kidnapping and murder of several young boys spanning the last twenty years," Chief Hurt said. "He is now in custody awaiting trial."

One reporter waved her hand. "What triggered his kidnapping spree?"

Chief Hurt indicated for Julie to take the question. "Mr. Moody suffered trauma while in combat overseas. When he returned his wife had left him and taken his little boy. Apparently when he couldn't find his son, he decided to replace him by kidnapping a boy named Jeremy. That was only the beginning. I can't divulge all the details, but the boy Jeremy is now in a psychiatric hospital undergoing evaluation and treatment."

More hands waved, voices shouting questions at Julie.

"What happened to the other boys he took?"

"Did he molest them?"

Julie held up a hand. "The boys were not sexually abused although they were definitely physically and emotionally abused. As Chief Hurt stated, we are not at liberty to divulge details, but all of the surviving victims have been reunited with their families, and are also undergoing extensive psychiatric evaluation and treatment."

Brody noticed Will's slight flinch and patted his back. "You're doing great, Will," he murmured. "You're the bravest guy I know."

Will slanted him one of those wary looks.

"How many victims were there?" another reporter asked.

"You said there are murder charges?" another one asked.

Julie's eyes flickered in pain then she grripped the podium. Brody saw the fatigue and anguish on her face, and wanted to drag her in his arms and comfort her. Dammit, she should be here with him and Will, not out there fighting monsters like Moody.

"Again, we cannot reveal details, but I can say that Moody kidnapped a total of ten victims. Sadly, we've recovered the bodies of four." She exhaled a labored breath. "On a positive note, that means we saved six lives. And the man who abducted and abused them is now awaiting trial."

She squared her shoulders. "So if you take anything away from this, folks, go home and love your children. Watch them, hug them, love them, and most of all know where they are."

Then she released the podium, dropped her head and walked away.

Chief Hurt stayed to answer more questions, but Brody stared at the screen, wanting more of Julie. Wanting her to be there with him.

"She's amazing," Will said.

Brody smiled, all his hesitations and rationalizations for not calling her fading away.

"You and she…you had a thing, didn't you?" Will asked.

Brody nodded.

"What happened?"

Brody shook his head. No way would he tell him that his disappearance had torn them apart.

It hadn't, he suddenly realized. He had torn them apart by not turning to the one person who had loved him most back then.

The question was—did she still love him, or had he hurt her too much to have a chance with her now?

Chapter Nineteen

Julie had to get away from the cameras. The last few days of interrogating Moody, of listening to the horror stories from the other victims had taken its toll.

She punched the elevator button inside the building, desperate to escape. Her chest hurt from trying to breathe, and for the first time in her life she thought she was going to have a panic attack.

She couldn't do this anymore.

Between the last case she'd worked, where women had been brutally slashed, and now this case, where so many children and families had had their lives destroyed by such a sick man, her trust in humanity was being slowly eaten away.

Guilt weighed on her. There were going to be more kids, more families, more women, more couples torn apart by some maniac.

When would it ever end?

It wouldn't. She couldn't save them all.

And that tormented her.

But you did save Will. And you brought him back to Brody.

As selfish as that was, for now, it might have to be enough.

Agent Cord rushed toward her, his expression concerned. "Are you okay, Julie?"

She fought back tears. "I…can't do it anymore, I have to get out."

His understanding nod somehow made the guilt slightly abate. "You did good, Julie. You did real good."

She pressed a hand to her mouth, swallowing back tears. If she started crying for all the victims she'd seen, all the horror she'd seen, she'd never stop crying.

"What will you do?" he asked softly.

"I don't know," she said, her voice cracking.

He sighed. "Julie, you love him. Go and tell him. Don't waste another seven years."

A laugh bubbled somewhere in the depths of her throat. Jay was such a good friend. And he was right.

"But what if I tell him and he doesn't feel the same way?" she whispered.

"My God, woman, you are a fool," he said with a smile. "The man loves you, and if he's too scared to admit it, remind him you stared down a bullet for him."

Julie nodded, blinking back tears, then hugged Jay just as the elevator dinged.

She would go to the BBL and see for herself.

After all, Brody had broken her heart seven years ago.

She wanted him to put it back together again.

Had he forgiven her for the past?

DUSK HAD JUST started to set when Brody realized he had to go to Julie.

Will was finishing dinner with some of the other guys, and he couldn't leave without telling him. He pulled him aside, wanting to make sure it was okay with his brother. After all, Will had only been back with him for a week. He was just adjusting, just getting used to his new life.

Trying to work through the past.

"Will, I... You were right about me and Julie," he said. "I was a fool to let her go, and I want to make it right."

Will arched a dark eyebrow. "What are you waiting for then?"

Brody shuffled on his feet, then pressed a hand to his brother's shoulder. "You," Brody said. "I've waited so long to have you back. I don't want to jeopardize our relationship—"

"Shut up and go get her," Will said with a teasing smile that warmed Brody's heart.

"You're sure?" Brody asked.

"Yeah, she's hot," Will said with a full grin this time.

Brody laughed for the first time in weeks. "Yeah, she is." He gave his brother a big hug, then jogged back to the main house.

His mind raced as he mentally made plans. He'd have to pack a bag in case he needed to stay overnight. Should he order flowers? Buy a ring?

Just as he stepped outside to go to his Jeep, a dark blue SUV rolled up. Brody frowned. He didn't recognize the vehicle.

Then the door opened, and Julie slid from the seat. She looked so beautiful that he could hardly stand it.

But worry quickly crept in. Had she come to tell him something more about the case? Had Moody escaped?

"Julie?"

"Hi, Brody," she said with a smile that looked so tentative his pulse hammerd.

"Where's your other car?" he asked, suddenly noting that she wasn't driving her FBI-issued black sedan.

She shrugged. "I turned it in and bought this."

It took him a moment for her statement to register. "You turned it in?"

"Yes, when I resigned." She shut the door, then walked toward him, a hint of the old Julie back. The flirty one who'd stolen his heart years ago.

"You resigned?"

She climbed the steps. "Yes. I don't know what I'm going to do now though."

The fact that she was here, that she'd left the job he hated, that she was smiling and wearing cowboy boots and jeans and a hat suddenly sank in, and hope budded in his chest.

"I know what you could do," he said as he reached for her and pulled her up against him.

Her gaze locked with his, a teasing playfulness lighting the depths that had been missing the last time he'd seen her. Of course, that had been when they were facing down Moody.

But he didn't want to think about Moody now. He wanted to enjoy the fact that Julie had come to him.

He nudged her cheek with his own, then whispered, "You could marry me."

Julie looped her arms around his neck and looked him in the eye, her face awash with the same love she'd shown him when she was just a girl. "I reckon I could do that," she said softly.

His heart stuttered. He was so damn happy he thought he would burst. "I love you," he said gruffly, then swung her up into his arms and twirled her around. "I've always loved you, Julie."

She threaded her fingers in his hair. "I love you, too, cowboy."

Then she closed her lips over his and kissed

him. "You won't mind if I don't work for a while?" she murmured when they came up for air.

"You can help me here on the BBL." He kissed her again. "And you can give me babies."

She threw her head back and laughed, a musical sound that warmed his heart. "How about we just start with one?"

"One sounds good to me," Brody said. "That is, for a start."

She laughed again, and he lifted her in his arms and carried her upstairs to the bedroom.

Epilogue

Julie had dreamed about a June wedding, and seven years after she'd talked about having it with Brody, it was finally coming true.

She had also dreamed about having a big family and between the boys at the BBL, Will, the men who ran the ranch and their wives, that was coming true, as well.

She and Johnny's wife, Rachel; Brandon's wife, Kim; Carter's wife, Sadie; Miles's wife, Jordan; and Mason's wife, Cara, had become like sisters. She waved to them all as they filed into their seats with their husbands. Rachel's son, Kenny, sat with Miles's son, Timmy, and Kim and Brandon's little girl, Lucy. Both Rachel and Kim were pregnant, and she'd heard Sadie, Cara and Jordan all talking about babies in the near future.

But the biggest surprise had been the phone call from her aunt. She had seen the news story featuring Julie and the abused boys, and finally decided to leave her husband. She said she'd taken the last beating of her life.

Julie had talked to Brody and like the honorable man and cowboy he was, he had offered her a place at the BBL. She was helping Ms. Ellen in the kitchen, and had blossomed under the other woman's loving care. Her uncle had come after her, but Brody had put the fear of God in him, and her uncle had slunk away. Between her warning and Brody's, they didn't expect to ever see him again.

Brody stood next to Will, his best man, beneath the same gazebo where Mason and Cara had married a few months ago. White chairs and ribbons adorned the outdoor festivities, with flowers adding color.

It turned out Agent Cord played the guitar and had offered to play for them.

It was a perfect spring day.

But it would have been perfect if it had been raining and there was no one here to watch, because she was marrying the perfect man.

Her cowboy and the love of her life.

Jay began strumming the wedding march, and she clutched her roses in one hand and started the bridal walk toward the man she loved.

And her soon-to-be husband.

BRODY HAD NEVER felt as blessed as he did on this day. Surrounded by his best friends, the ranch hands, counselors and kids on the BBL, and his brother, life just couldn't get any better.

Sunlight painted a radiant picture of his bride as she walked toward him, the golden light shimmering off her simple but elegant wedding dress.

"She's great, Brody," Will whispered. "Someday I hope I find a girl like her."

Brody choked back emotions. The fact that Will was looking ahead was a good sign. "You will one day, Will. And she is wonderful. I wouldn't have you back if she hadn't kept looking the way she did." He loved her even more for that.

Because she had sacrificed her dreams for him.

He would make sure she followed her own dreams from now on. Hell, if she still wanted to go to vet school, he'd pay for that.

Or if she wanted to have babies and raise a family, he was all over that, too.

Still, Will was the amazing one. He was not only making great strides in his own recovery but also opening up and helping others. He and the boys who'd survived shared their own special bond and Brody had welcomed them onto the ranch as part of the family.

The guitar music faded as Julie took his hand, and the reverend began the ceremony. Ten minutes later, he walked his wife down the aisle and the celebration began.

Food, champagne and cake added to the party,

then the music started again and Brody swept Julie onto the makeshift dance floor for their first dance as man and wife.

She wrapped her arms around his neck and kissed him again as he swung her around. "I love you, Brody."

"I love you, too," he whispered. "Forever and always."

She smiled into his eyes. "Forever and always."

Then Brody looked across the dance floor and saw Will smiling. He returned the smile, so proud of him he wanted to shout it to the heavens.

Moody had taken him away seven years ago, but Julie had brought him back.

She and Will were both heroes.

And he had no doubt that one day his brother would take over the BBL and continue the work that he had started.

* * * * *

LARGER-PRINT BOOKS!
GET 2 FREE LARGER-PRINT NOVELS PLUS 2 FREE GIFTS!

♦HARLEQUIN®

INTRIGUE®

BREATHTAKING ROMANTIC SUSPENSE

YES! Please send me 2 FREE LARGER-PRINT Harlequin Intrigue® novels and my 2 FREE gifts (gifts are worth about $10). After receiving them, if I don't wish to receive any more books, I can return the shipping statement marked "cancel." If I don't cancel, I will receive 6 brand-new novels every month and be billed just $5.24 per book in the U.S. or $5.99 per book in Canada. That's a saving of at least 13% off the cover price! It's quite a bargain! Shipping and handling is just 50¢ per book in the U.S. and 75¢ per book in Canada.* I understand that accepting the 2 free books and gifts places me under no obligation to buy anything. I can always return a shipment and cancel at any time. Even if I never buy another book, the two free books and gifts are mine to keep forever.

199/399 HDN FVQ7

Name (PLEASE PRINT)

Address   Apt. #

City   State/Prov.   Zip/Postal Code

Signature (if under 18, a parent or guardian must sign)

Mail to the **Harlequin® Reader Service:**
IN U.S.A.: P.O. Box 1867, Buffalo, NY 14240-1867
IN CANADA: P.O. Box 609, Fort Erie, Ontario L2A 5X3

Are you a subscriber to Harlequin Intrigue books and want to receive the larger-print edition?
Call 1-800-873-8635 today or visit www.ReaderService.com.

* Terms and prices subject to change without notice. Prices do not include applicable taxes. Sales tax applicable in N.Y. Canadian residents will be charged applicable taxes. Offer not valid in Quebec. This offer is limited to one order per household. Not valid for current subscribers to Harlequin Intrigue Larger-Print books. All orders subject to credit approval. Credit or debit balances in a customer's account(s) may be offset by any other outstanding balance owed by or to the customer. Please allow 4 to 6 weeks for delivery. Offer available while quantities last.

Your Privacy—The Harlequin® Reader Service is committed to protecting your privacy. Our Privacy Policy is available online at www.ReaderService.com or upon request from the Harlequin Reader Service.

We make a portion of our mailing list available to reputable third parties that offer products we believe may interest you. If you prefer that we not exchange your name with third parties, or if you wish to clarify or modify your communication preferences, please visit us at www.ReaderService.com/consumerschoice or write to us at Harlequin Reader Service Preference Service, P.O. Box 9062, Buffalo, NY 14269. Include your complete name and address.

HILP13

ReaderService.com

Manage your account online!
- Review your order history
- Manage your payments
- Update your address

---

*We've designed
the Harlequin® Reader Service
website just for you.*

Enjoy all the features!
- Reader excerpts from any series
- Respond to mailings and special monthly offers
- Discover new series available to you
- Browse the Bonus Bucks catalog
- Share your feedback

Visit us at:

ReaderService.com

REQUEST YOUR FREE BOOKS!

2 FREE NOVELS
PLUS 2 FREE GIFTS!

Your Partner in Crime

YES! Please send me 2 FREE novels from the Worldwide Library® series and my 2 FREE gifts (gifts are worth about $10). After receiving them, if I don't wish to receive any more books, I can return the shipping statement marked "cancel." If I don't cancel, I will receive 4 brand-new novels every month and be billed just $5.24 per book in the U.S. or $6.24 per book in Canada. That's a savings of at least 34% off the cover price. It's quite a bargain! Shipping and handling is just 50¢ per book in the U.S. and 75¢ per book in Canada.* I understand that accepting the 2 free books and gifts places me under no obligation to buy anything. I can always return a shipment and cancel at any time. Even if I never buy another book, the two free books and gifts are mine to keep forever.

414/424 WDN FVUV

Name	(PLEASE PRINT)	
Address		Apt. #
City	State/Prov.	Zip/Postal Code

Signature (if under 18, a parent or guardian must sign)

Mail to the Harlequin® Reader Service:
IN U.S.A.: P.O. Box 1867, Buffalo, NY 14240-1867
IN CANADA: P.O. Box 609, Fort Erie, Ontario L2A 5X3

Want to try two free books from another line?
Call 1-800-873-8635 or visit www.ReaderService.com.

* Terms and prices subject to change without notice. Prices do not include applicable taxes. Sales tax applicable in N.Y. Canadian residents will be charged applicable taxes. Offer not valid in Quebec. This offer is limited to one order per household. Not valid for current subscribers to the Worldwide Library series. All orders subject to credit approval. Credit or debit balances in a customer's account(s) may be offset by any other outstanding balance owed by or to the customer. Please allow 4 to 6 weeks for delivery. Offer available while quantities last.

Your Privacy—The Harlequin® Reader Service is committed to protecting your privacy. Our Privacy Policy is available online at www.ReaderService.com or upon request from the Harlequin Reader Service.

We make a portion of our mailing list available to reputable third parties that offer products we believe may interest you. If you prefer that we not exchange your name with third parties, or if you wish to clarify or modify your communication preferences, please visit us at www.ReaderService.com/consumerschoice or write to us at Harlequin Reader Service Preference Service, P.O. Box 9062, Buffalo, NY 14269. Include your complete name and address.

WWLI3